Will Power!

He was a class clown turned rap star whose teachers nicknamed him "The Prince" because he could smooth-talk his way out of anything.

By his eighteenth birthday, he was a millionaire with a Grammy Award for Best Rap Single. He had already tasted success, but he wanted more.

He fulfilled his long desire to act by starring in the hit series *The Fresh Prince of Bel Air,* which ran for six years.

Turning his sights to the big screen, he set out to make his mark in blockbuster movies such as *Independence Day, Bad Boys,* and *Men in Black,* becoming one of Hollywood's hottest new stars.

What's he like? What does he like? Who does he hang with and where? Is this Philly boy a true Prince? Read on . . .

WILL SMITH!

A Biography of Will Smith,

Jan Berenson

AN ARCHWAY PAPERBACK
Published by POCKET BOOKS
New York London Toronto Sydney Tokyo Singapore

AN ARCHWAY PAPERBACK *Original*

An Archway Paperback published by
POCKET BOOKS, a division of Simon & Schuster Inc.
1230 Avenue of the Americas, New York, NY 10020

ISBN: 0-671-88784-X

First Archway Paperback printing May 1997

10 9 8 7 6 5 4 3

AN ARCHWAY PAPERBACK and colophon are registered trademarks of Simon & Schuster Inc.

Front cover photo by Braun/Outline Press Syndicate; back cover photo by Estrine/Outline Press Syndicate

Printed in the U.S.A.

IL: 5+

Acknowledgments

The author wishes to acknowledge the contributions of these people:

Lisa Clancy, at Archway Paperbacks, for all her support and help.

Stacey Woolf; JM for the tireless research; MM for her "you, go girl!" attitude; KW for never saying "no" to any request—you all are the best. And to the pillars, you know who you are, love always.

Contents

Contents

Introduction

"My life is just really, really great," reflects Will
Smith. Fact is, it pretty much always has been. An
American dream, you could call it.

Willard Smith, Jr., was a rap star before high
school graduation, a Grammy winner and millionaire by his twenty-first birthday. But that was just
for starters. During his first trip to Hollywood, he
snared his own TV comedy series. *The Fresh Prince
of Bel Air* ran for six successful years and is now, in
perpetual reruns, an authentic television icon.

Then came movies—make that, blockbuster
movies like *Bad Boys, Independence Day, Men in
Black*. Will Smith, well before his thirtieth birthday, is one of today's hugest, most bankable action
movie heroes.

More important, perhaps, he's done it all by smashing stereotypes and managing to stay squarely in the hearts of the American public. Simply put, people like Will Smith. He makes us laugh; he's made us care about his screen characters and about himself. We feel for him, we laugh with him, we root for him.

How lucky can you get? Will would be the first to admit that luck has been a major player in his life. But so have equal measures of pluck, smarts, savvy, and serious determination. He's as wily as he is wild 'n' crazy; as responsible as he seems irreverent; as methodical as he acts manic.

Will Smith's story is as much about faith, family, and the firm belief in honesty, loyalty, taking responsibility for his mistakes, and learning from them as it is about luck. It's an inspirational tale of accomplishment: It starts now.

Chapter 1

Where There's a Will!

When Will Smith was growing up in Philadelphia, he never dreamed he'd become one of the movies' biggest action stars. The idea that he'd be famous all over the world never occurred to him, and certainly he never thought he'd one day command millions of dollars for each new movie. But all the traits that got him exactly where he is today were evident early on. Everything he is now—funny, charming, talented, creative, musical, ambitious, diligent, smart, and self-confident—he was from the get-go.

Will Smith has always commanded the spotlight, even when the audience comprised just the six people in his immediate family. He has always been an actor, acting cool, acting the cut-up, acting his way out of touchy situations, well before he ever got a paycheck for it. He has always been self-confident, a trait that sometimes came off as grandiosity, but has, in fact, seen him through a lot of down times. He has always had the drive to be the best at whatever he did, and the will power to see it through. He has always been able to roll with the punches, and learn from them. And when it comes to reinventing himself, few performers have done it more convincingly.

Most important, perhaps, Will Smith has always been, deep down, a good person, someone who strives to do the right thing. That genuine sweetness translated via albums, TV screens, and movie screens has taken him straight into the hearts of millions of fans.

Will Smith has never pretended to be anything he wasn't. He has always been honest about his roots, his influences, his values, even when they didn't exactly go with his "image." He started out as a rap singer, but he never was "from the streets," nor did he ever say he was. Instead, he was from a loving, solid, hardworking family, who not only encouraged Will to develop his natural talents, but guided him—lovingly and firmly—every step of the way. No one ever planned for Will to become a star; but in so many ways, it couldn't have been planned better. Everything he did as a kid led right up to it.

Willard Smith, Jr., was born on September 25, 1968, to Caroline and Willard Smith, Sr., who were already parents to a daughter named Pamela. A few years after Will Junior's birth, the family was complete with the arrival of the twins, Harry and Ellen. The Smiths lived in a brick row house in Winfield, a neighborhood in southwest Philadelphia. The area was solidly working-class; neither wealthy nor impoverished. Will's family, who lived by the words "You get up in the morning prepared to go to work," fit right in. Caroline and Will Senior believed in the value of hard work. Will's mom spent her career as an administrator for the local board of education. His dad owned and operated Arcac, a refrigeration firm. He designed, installed, and repaired the refrigeration units found in supermarkets. Despite being active, working parents, the Smiths didn't miss a beat when it came to the education or the behavior of their kids. They were right on top of it all.

Will was a sweet-tempered baby whose smile could light up the galaxy. Not surprisingly, he was also a motor-mouth. "He could talk before he could walk," his mom remembers fondly. But little Will could be a good listener, too, as long as his parents were reading his favorite books aloud. As a toddler, he especially loved the lilting and clever rhymes in the Dr. Seuss books. In fact, they made a lasting impression on him. Years later Will would attribute his affinity for rap rhymes to those books. "If you listen to them a certain way, books like *Green Eggs and Ham* and *Hop on Pop* sound a lot like hip-hop," he once said.

As a little guy, Will discovered his own gift for making up original stories and entertaining his family. An extra bonus was all the attention this innate talent sent his way. "It's always been fun for me to tell a story and make people laugh. I've always been a show-off. I only got uncomfortable when people *weren't* looking at me," he admits. Lucky for him—and eventually for his fans—his family *was* looking, laughing, *and* encouraging his creative, if sometimes wacky, side. To be fair, however, Will wasn't the only cutup kid *or* adult of the clan. "I was blessed with a really, really funny family," he reveals. "Dinnertime was like a nightly laugh riot."

Still, it was always silly Will who pushed the laugh riots over the top sometimes. "Will did the gross things kids do, like put straws up his nose," his sister Ellen recalled. And though his parents saw the humor in much of his innocent mischief, they drew the line at misbehavior. "Will was punished first because he's older than me and Harry, and because he usually started things," Ellen told, "but then he'd do something like make faces that would crack us up—and we'd end up getting punished worse."

Along with the nightly banter, there was always music in Will's home. He had his first stereo system before he was ten—a gift from Dad—on which he mostly listened to albums by groups like Parliament Funkadelic and the Bar-kays. But music was never just a passive activity chez Smith: Will and everyone in the family sang and were encouraged to play an instrument. The clan even formed a little jazz band at one point.

"There were instruments around the house, and I just played a little of everything," Will explained, noting that he picked up drums on his own, and piano from his mom, who used to play the music of her favorite composer, Beethoven. A decade later, in a scene from the very first episode of *The Fresh Prince of Bel Air,* Will unexpectedly sat down at the piano and tapped out the Beethoven composition *Für Elise.* That wasn't in the script, just something Will improvised that came straight out of his childhood memories.

Will's grandmother, Helen Bright, lived nearby. She was a frequent visitor and profound influence on his life. A leader at her church, she used to organize the Easter egg hunts and put together plays and holiday programs. In that capacity, she was responsible for Will's first foray on stage. "My grandmother put us all in her little plays at Resurrection Baptist Church," Will remembers. For a boy admittedly most at home in the spotlight, performing on stage felt completely natural. He liked that first taste of it.

But performing in church wasn't the only reason for Will's attendance; command performances every Sunday were a way of life for him and his siblings. And that, he later admitted, was a good thing. "You have to believe in something greater than yourself. You have to have faith in the power and believe it has your best interest at heart. That's how I was raised by my parents, and that's the bottom line."

The feeling that "there's something greater than yourself" was further instilled during a family vacation when Will was only seven years old. It's a trip etched in his memory. "We drove cross-country and saw natural wonders of the world, like Yellowstone National Park and the Grand Canyon. We went to historical sights like Mt. Rushmore and the Alamo," Will once related. "When you see something beautiful, something bigger than you, whether it's created by nature or by man, it changes you, it mellows you, it changes your attitude for life."

Of course, Will wasn't so changed that he stopped being funny. Instead, as he grew, his knack for comedy and penchant for storytelling sharpened. He honed his skills watching TV. His favorite shows were comedies like *Happy Days, Laverne & Shirley,* and *Three's Company;* he'd watch them without fail every week. He also liked the slightly edgier, more adult comedies *Taxi* (which starred, among others, Danny DeVito and Tony Danza) and *Soap* (among its ensemble cast was Billy Crystal), but he had to watch them on the sly—his parents felt they were on past his bedtime and a little risqué for him.

Will's all-time favorite star wasn't on TV, though. The phenomenally successful movie comic Eddie Murphy was the young boy's idol, and Will saw every one of Eddie's films that he was allowed to, including *Trading Places* and *Beverly Hills Cop.* "Eddie is a genius, that was something I instinctively knew," Will has acknowledged.

Still, all during his early growing-up years, Will never seriously considered following in his idol's laugh track. Showbiz was simply out of his realm, and therefore not a career option. He enjoyed entertaining people and was good at it; that was clear. "He always had an energy that drew people to him," his sister admitted. He enjoyed and appreciated being entertained, that was also clear. But had he been asked, back in elementary school, what he wanted to be when he grew up, little Will Smith would surely not have said "movie star." He wouldn't have said "rap star," or "TV star," or mentioned performing as a way of making a living, let alone the path to superstardom. Instead, he considered his natural talents just a part of who he was.

The truth is, Will wasn't exactly sure of what he wanted to be when he grew up. He did know that whatever he chose, he had to be the best at it—and would take it to the extreme. "I wasn't the kind of kid who dreamed about being a fireman or policeman," he once explained. "I wanted to go up in the space shuttle."

Will attended Our Lady of Lourdes Elementary School from kindergarten through eighth grade. He was a good student and showed promise in a variety of subjects. He excelled at math and science and thought briefly about becoming a computer engineer. He was also a top English student, especially when it came to creative writing. He wrote poetry, too, and was rewarded with praise and good grades for his efforts. "I was good at it, so I kept at it," he explains.

He was just as good, however, at being the class clown. That gift endeared him to his classmates, who found his goofy humor irresistible. Unsurprisingly, Will was quite comfortable with the class clown tag and worked it. He's never said so in so many words, but it's also possible that the young boy believed humor was the key to his popularity. Certainly, he never felt anyone was drawn to him because of his good looks; how could he? "When I was little, everybody always told me I looked like Alfred E. Newman, the weird guy on the cover of *Mad Magazine,*" Will has said. "I always had that square-looking fade hairdo, and I liked it, even though it made my ears stick out. One guy once told me I looked like a car with the doors open."

Will used humor to open the doors of friendship and to keep the spotlight where he liked it—squarely on him. But there was a fine line between being the class cutup and a real troublemaker. Will understood exactly where the line was—somewhere on the way home from school, in fact—and never crossed it. The school goofball never raised his voice to his parents or disrespected them in any way. "You might get your face slapped" was the main reason why.

In fact, Will managed to resist getting into any serious trouble, no matter which friends might be influencing him. "Even with peer pressure, there wasn't a friend I had who could pressure me to do something I knew would get me into trouble with my father. My father had so much control over me when I was growing up—I didn't have too much of an opportunity to do things the wrong way. My father was always in my business. He always knew everything I was doing! He was always there to make sure I knew what the right way was. He was the man with all the answers, the disciplinarian. He did his shaping up by taking little chunks out of your behind!" There is no anger in Will's voice: That's just the way it was, and he accepted it.

In spite of being firm disciplinarians, Will's folks always made their love and support for their kids abundantly clear. Which is why, even after all these years, they remain his heroes. "There are individual personality traits of celebrities and sports stars I admire, but the only people I continue to idolize are my parents. They taught me clearly the difference between right and wrong, and that when you make a mistake, you must be honest with yourself about it."

When Will was thirteen, his parents followed their own advice and were honest with him, Pam, Harry, and Ellen: They told the kids they were divorcing. While it must have come as a shock, unsettling at the very least, Will has always maintained a respectful silence about whatever events led up to it. More important, from his point of view, he and his siblings emerged as unscathed as humanly possible. "We never felt our parents didn't love us," Will told about that time in their lives. "No matter how difficult things got, or how angry someone might have gotten, no matter what happened in our lives, we always felt like we had somewhere to go." For that, more than anything, Will is thankful. "You can't spring off into the world from a flimsy base, you've got to have a solid base to jump from. My parents, together or apart, provided that base."

Although he continued to live with his mom, he

maintained very close ties with his dad and saw him nearly as much as when they all lived together. During Will's middle school years, he worked for his dad every day after school, installing and repairing refrigerators. One particular day after work, instead of taking him straight home, Will's dad took a detour through the skid row section of Philadelphia. "He pointed to the bums sleeping in the doorways and said, 'This is what people look like when they do drugs.'" That was all Will ever had to see or hear. He never went near drugs.

Will Senior sought to inspire his sons, too. One summer he insisted that Will Junior and Harry tear down and then rebuild a brick wall that was deteriorating. The brothers worked all summer at it. They weren't finished in the fall, so after school and on weekends, for several more months, they went back until they finally completed the arduous task. When they were done, they weren't rewarded with money, but with something even more valuable: words of wisdom. "Now, don't ever tell me you can't do something." Will never forgot that. "I look back on a lot of times in my life when I think I won't be able to do something. Then I think about that wall, and tell myself, 'one brick at a time.'"

Clearly, Will has always taken his dad's advice seriously, including this tidbit: "If you just do one thing well, make sure you can focus, and everything else will come from that."

When Will Senior said it, however, it's doubtful he ever thought his son would apply it to . . . rap music. But one day in 1979, when Will was only eleven, he heard a song on the radio. It changed the course of his life. The song was "Rapper's Delight," by the Sugar Hill Gang. Not only did Will groove to its hip-hop beat, the song inspired a powerful realization: "They weren't doing anything I couldn't do."

Chapter 2

The Clown Prince of Overbrook High

Will's early teen years coincided with the exciting beginnings of rap music. And he was instantly intrigued, as was nearly every other teenager he knew. "When rap came out," Will's future partner Jeff Townes once explained, "there was this buzz: *This* is something new. We never heard this before, but somebody made this especially for us. This is *our* music because our parents don't like it, our grandmothers don't like it. But *we* like it."

Rap was everywhere. Will once explained, "When you grow up in any urban area, particularly a black area, you can't escape it. Rap is the urban music. Everybody in the street is a rapper, or a DJ, or a beat box. Hip-hop is a culture. It's not just music, it's a way of life."

It soon became *the* way for Will. In fact, it was the perfect combination of his two loves: making up stories and music. And Will was admittedly consumed by the new form. "I started rapping just as soon as I heard that first song. I rapped all day long until I thought my mom was going to lose her mind! Music, after all, has always been in my heart. At first, I did it as a hobby, and I enjoyed it and got really good at it. When you enjoy what you do, you're going to get really good at it. And I just concentrated on it."

It wouldn't remain a hobby for long.

Part of rap culture involves competing, and back in the late seventies, street corners in cities all over America were suddenly host to informal "I can do it better than you, check *this* out," rap competitions. It surprised no one that spotlight-hugger Will dived right in. Of course, he was good at it. "My reputation came from beating other rappers in street challenges. I never lost a street battle," Will once boasted.

Street corners weren't the only place for rappers to strut their stuff. In many areas block parties became the central focus of community social life. Those parties had to have music: It was inevitably supplied by a homegrown DJ (someone who creatively spun and scratched the music) and a rapper, whose original verses were often challenged by others at the party.

Partly because he had absorbed his parents' work ethic—and mostly because he just liked it—Will wasn't long content just composing, performing, and competing with his little rap songs on the corner of his neighborhood. Nor was he going to be content at being anything less than the best. "I was going to all those block parties, having fun and competing with my raps. It suddenly occurred to me, 'okay, if I'm going to party, I might as well get paid for it.'" Which is how Will became . . . a DJ, actually, at first. No longer just a guest at neighborhood parties, Will first earned money spinning the records. His silent stint behind the turntable didn't last long, however: Will's natural way with words won over. The boy couldn't contain himself, he had to bust out and be the rapper. At all the subsequent parties he worked, that's exactly what he was. In the space of a few months Will had earned a reputation as one of southwest Philadelphia's freshest new hip-hoppers. He was all of thirteen years old.

Time out. Most people who know something about Will Smith's early history as a rapper would predict that his historic meeting with Jeff Townes—aka DJ Jazzy Jeff—comes in right about now. But that's not exactly how it happened. Will actually formed another rap outfit first. A duo, it consisted of himself and his friend, "the human beat box," Clarence "Clate" Holmes, whose "nom de rap" was Ready Rock-C. And somewhere during the time he and Ready Rock-C were doing their thing, it dawned on Will that perhaps there was a future in this for him. He'd been listening to such cutting-edge rap stars as Crash Crew, Kurtis Blow, Busy Bee, and Cold Crush Brothers. Moreover, he'd never forgotten the Sugar Hill Gang's song. That feeling he had three years earlier—"They weren't doing anything I couldn't do"—had never left him. In fact, it was stronger than ever.

With a fistful of material written by Will and performed by himself and Ready Rock-C, he approached a well-known rap producer named Dana Goodman, who was responsible for signing local acts to the independent, but successful, Word Up record label. Although the producer was impressed with Will's songs, there just weren't enough of them to fill an entire CD. He was told to "go home and get more material." And he was just about to, when fate stepped in: *That's* when he met Jeff!

The story of how and when Will Smith first met Jeff Townes has become almost legendary. Although it's hardly ever been told the same way twice, one fact remains immutable. That meeting changed the course of both their lives forever: Because of it, they veered smack into the fast lane of success.

Jeff Townes came from southwest Philadelphia, not far from Will's neighborhood, and he, too, was immediately hooked on rap. By his own account, he started working parties at the age of ten. "I used to call myself a bathroom DJ," he once quipped, "because I would tag along to parties with older DJs and finally get my chance to go on when they went to the bathroom!"

All kidding aside, Jeff worked hard, and by and large taught himself the art of being a rap DJ. Since Jeff had always been into jazz, one of his ideas was to fuse that musical genre with hip-hop. He set up his basement as a mini recording studio and worked on doing just that. He toyed with techniques like catching double beats, scratching two records at once, back-spinning, and "transforming" (taking a sound already on record and altering it to sound like something completely different.)

After a while Jeff got the opportunity to debut his new sound on a local radio station. He was instantly the talk of the nascent rap nation. Suddenly it seemed as if the entire Philadelphia rap community wanted him for gigs. Jeff immediately dubbed himself "DJ Jazzy Jeff" and by 1983 was flying high as one of the top hip-hop DJs around. He was all of seventeen.

Of course, a DJ needs a crew: a rapper and a beat box, and over the next several years, Jeff hooked up with several different units. But none ever jelled just right. It would take a full three years for that to happen.

The year was 1986, the month, January, the place, a party in Will Smith's neighborhood. In fact, it was on his block. As Jeff recalled in an article in *Disney Adventures,* "I was the best DJ in Philadelphia and I had heard of Will, but I already had someone that I worked with. But when I played that party on Will's block, naturally he was there. He asked if he could rap for a while and I said yes. He started rapping and I started cutting, and it was like natural chemistry. He flowed with what I did and I flowed exactly with what he did and we knew it. We just clicked the whole night long. The chemistry between us was so good. I went home and dreamed about him. I got his number and we got together."

Clearly, Jeff had strong feelings about a partnership with Will, but because of his bad luck with so many previous crews, he wasn't completely convinced he'd found the right rapper. One might say that the whole deal didn't "smell" totally right to Jeff—that would take a can of something called "PU." "A few weeks after we met," Jeff explains, "we were working a party together. I bought this canned fart spray called PU, and as a goof, sprayed it at the party. I cracked up, and so did Will. That's when I realized we were down with the same humor. That's when we really clicked."

It was a "click," in fact, that neither had ever experienced with any other fellow musicians. "We were laughing and joking like we'd known each other for ten years." Jeff had another realization after that night: "Together, we could be the ultimate, not just in Philadelphia, but everywhere: Nobody could touch us."

The pair started working together steadily, playing not only parties, but church functions and clubs. Their musical melding turned out to be only part of what they did. They incorporated their humor into the act from the start. "We had a pretty new style that people were finding interesting," Will reported, "plus, we could make people laugh at a party scene."

They also incorporated something else into their act: Ready Rock-C on the beat box. Will has never been someone to drop a friend just because a better opportunity came along. He didn't then, and he

wouldn't later on, as Jeff would be the first to testify
to. Will is a good person at heart; he always has
been.

As consumed as Will was with rap, and as
successful and well-known as he and Jeff were
becoming, music didn't take up all his time. It
couldn't. Will was, after all, only sixteen and still in
high school. There was no way his parents were
about to let his musical hobby—lucrative though it
was beginning to be—interfere with his education.
That was never going to happen.

In ninth grade Will enrolled in Overbrook High.
Quickly he established his rep there. It wasn't very
different from the one he'd had at Our Lady of
Lourdes: class clown. "I was just silly all the time,"
Will admitted. "People I went to school with
probably remember me as a jackass."

The class clown found his ability to compose on
the spot very handy in school. Will was good, really
good, at talking his way out of trouble. "I always
used to get into silly trouble, but I was always so
charming, I could smooth talk my way out of any
situation." A missed assignment, a less than stellar
grade on a paper, cutting up in the classroom,
whatever—Will always had an excuse. Unlike the
lame ones offered up by his classmates, Will's were
always original, creative, usually funny, and so
heartfelt that most of his teachers didn't punish
him. Instead, they gave him a nickname: Prince
Charming.

Making excuses was only part of what "the
Prince," as he soon became widely known, did.
The truth is, Will really did work hard in high

school. "I'd cut up in class, but still take in what the teacher was saying," he's insisted.

He continued to be a top English student, writing poetry and reading Edgar Allan Poe; he caught on easily to math and science. He even, for a term, played in the school band. Will's high school grades, while not spectacular, were still solid. His head was in the books just enough; his heart was elsewhere.

Looking back, Will reflects, "I got the grades mainly to please my parents. I didn't think I'd ever use what I learned. But in my rap and as an actor, it's amazing how much of what I did learn comes back to me. It all pays off in the end. I just didn't know that then."

What he did know, and what most of Philadelphia was starting to know, was that he and Jeff were poised to take off. Will had never given up on the idea of making a record; Jeff was one step ahead of him. Before meeting Will, he'd actually *had* a solo record out, but it flopped. Now that they were a team, the goal was clear. The pair described it in typical rap grandiosity. "Our destiny was to be the most versatile group to come out of rap." Naturally, to meet that "destiny," they needed to be heard—and for that, they needed a record deal. They got to work, every weekend, and after school, spending hours making tapes in Jeff's mini recording studio, still located in his basement. The natural division, of course, was for Jeff to write the music, Will the lyrics. "We'd sit down and talk about things first. The songs come from our own experiences." When they were ready to put it on tape, Will would say a verse, and Jeff would add the beat. They'd throw it back and forth until they had it down.

Because Will had already been dubbed "the Prince" in school, and so many people knew him by that nickname, he decided to use it as part of his rap name. He added "Fresh" because "at the time, the word *Fresh* was *the* word," Will explained. "It was street talk for cool, the best." Together, he and Jeff officially became, "DJ Jazzy Jeff and the Fresh Prince."

And so it was under that name, they submitted the best of their original demo tapes to Dana Goodman, the same rap producer who had turned Will away several years earlier. This time the answer was radically, and speedily different. Dana signed up the group to the independent Word Up record label. The first twelve-inch single released on it was a tongue-in-cheek ditty about the perils of teen romance called "Girls Ain't Nothing But Trouble."

While very much a hip-hop tune, the song was admittedly different from the normal rap of the day, as exemplified by the hard-edged Public Enemy and N.W.A. But "Girls" was also very typical of DJ Jazzy Jeff and the Fresh Prince. It wasn't angry; it wasn't "street." Instead, it was true to who the boys were: lighthearted, high-spirited, and funny. It was also an immediate smash and soon spread from local Philadelphia radio station play to rap radio all across the country. In fact, it hip-hopped over the Atlantic Ocean, and became a Top 20 hit in England. A whoosh of sales soon followed, to the tune of 100,000 copies, and Will and Jeff began their odyssey of what they'd call "livin' large."

The summer after "Girls Ain't Nothing But Trouble" hit, they were invited to join the Def Jam tour along with major rap stars like LL Cool J, Eric B. & Rakim, Public Enemy, and Whodini. London, England, was one of the stops on the tour. When they landed there, Jeff and the Prince were treated royally. Will recalls: "There were screaming girls at the airport, and we just thought, 'What is this? What are they screaming for?'"

To someone else, the whole trip—the record, the tour, the fans—might have seemed like some pipe dream magically coming true, but Will and Jeff didn't react that way. For Will, it was simply proof that his instincts were right on target. He really could, in fact, do it better than the Sugar Hill Gang and others on the radio. For Jeff, who'd been working at rap for ten years, the sweet turn of events seemed a natural progression.

Along with that first flush of success, however, was something they didn't anticipate, or feel natural about: the first heat of criticism. "Girls" was immediately attacked, on not one but two fronts. Some journalists declared the song "sexist." Will, who'd grown up with nothing but respect for his mother, sisters, and grandmother, was stung. He lashed out quickly. "That's a ridiculous, idiotic opinion," he slammed back at the song's detractors. "The rap is a personal story, told with a sense of humor, rather than a statement of general attitude." Still, just for fun (from Will's point of view), but perhaps as an apology (as it was perceived in the music press), DJ Jazzy Jeff and the Fresh Prince did record an "answer" song (with a female rapper) called *"Guys* Ain't Nothing But Trouble!"

The other bit of criticism wasn't so easy to shake off. From the get-go, the duo was slammed by the hard-core rap community for being too soft. The barbs were bitter and relentless. As were Will's and Jeff's constant defending of their music. The successes, and the slings and arrows aimed at them because of it, would follow them for the next decade.

Certainly, success upon success piled on, with increasing speed. DJ Jazzy Jeff and the Fresh Prince quickly moved from that independent label to a major, Jive Records. It was on that label, in 1987, that their first album came out.

Rock the House was its title. All the tracks on it were pure DJ Jazzy Jeff and the Fresh Prince—not angry, not "street," but extremely clever and just plain fun. "Just One of Those Days," with its chorus, "Have you ever in your life experienced a day/Where nothing at all seems to go your way?" was the kind of song everyone could relate to. "The Magnificent Jazzy Jeff" praised Jeff's talents to "cut up records like a Samurai warrior." "Takin' It to the Top," on which Will warbled, "Ain't a rapper with the rhyme, as impressive as mine," was tongue-in-cheek boastful. The title track, as they proudly announced in their first press release, was written by the group's "extra special associate member," Ready Rock-C, "the human beat box," who certainly hadn't been left behind by Will and Jeff.

Rock the House might not have been "street," but that's exactly where it was successful. It sold an impressive 600,000 copies, enough to qualify as a gold record.

The sales, the accolades, the tour, the money: It all added up to the biggest dilemma of Will Smith's young life—his first real "battle of wills" with his parents.

For *Rock the House* was clearly about to lead to another album, another tour. Bigger things were clearly on tap for the pair. Only it all came down during Will's senior year of high school, the year he should have been, according to his parents, thinking about college. Will tried hard to juggle what his parents wanted him to do with what he already *was* doing, and loving.

His grades actually improved that last year, not because Will got serious about school, but because his mom did. "My guidance counselor called my mom and told her that I was testing at college level, but my grades did not reflect it." Will had to buckle down and he did.

He even took the college aptitude test. "I had really high SAT scores," he reveals. That led to interviews for various colleges and, because his parents expected him to, actual applications filed. One school that accepted him immediately was the Milwaukee School of Engineering. It has also been widely reported that Will, in fact, turned down a scholarship to the prestigious MIT (Massachusetts

Institute of Technology), but it turns out he never said exactly that. What he said—in *US Magazine*—is this: "I was talking to the guys [recruiters] from MIT, and there was some kind of two-year pre-engineering prep course that they were interested in having me apply for." Only he never did apply. Instead, he finally confronted his mom and told her the truth. He had no intention of following through and going to MIT, or anyplace else. "This guy at MIT sounds really nice," is Will's recollection of the conversation, "but I want to be a rapper. I think I can do that."

Will's mom reacted . . . not serenely. "She had a conniption" is how Will remembers it. Eventually, partly due to Will's powers of persuasion, and his budding success, Caroline Smith agreed to a compromise. "She let me talk to my father, who was also none too thrilled with the course of events. Still, my father basically said, 'Okay. Take a year [to continue with rap]. If it works, God bless you. If it doesn't, you'll go to college.'"

Chapter 3

Livin' Large—and Falling Far

Will Smith never did go to college. Instead, he immersed himself in another kind of higher education: real life, showbiz style. Along with Jeff, he dived right in, headfirst, experiencing the dizzying heights of success; to be followed, more quickly than he would have believed possible, by the terrifying, lonely "how'd this happen?" lows.

It all started on a high note, and just after high school graduation. That's when Will and Jeff went to work on album number two. They wanted to put out a record so extreme, it would set them up as kings of the genre. It took eighteen long months to accomplish, but in the end they kind of did exactly that.

Their sophomore effort, released in 1988, was

titled *He's the DJ, I'm the Rapper*. Like *Rock the House*, this new album reflected Will and Jeff's irreverent sense of humor and flippant approach to everyday life. It wasn't so much hip-hop as flip-hop!

That said, still *He's the DJ, I'm the Rapper* showed enormous growth of the "def duo." First of all, it was a two-record set, the first of any rap album to contain that many tracks. But it wasn't just more music, it was better music. The critically acclaimed songs continued to be inspired by Will's and Jeff's personal experiences. "Here We Go Again" explained what took so long between albums. They wrote ". . . it takes a long time to travel the globe/the last album was def . . . and here we go again."

In "Nightmare on My Street," Jeff paid homage to his favorite *Nightmare on Elm Street* horror films. Then there was "Let's Get Busy Baby," in which Will offered his "dating dos and don'ts." Will rapped about the partnership between himself and Jeff in "Brand New Funk."

The track that jumped off the album, however, was "Parents Just Don't Understand." To this day, it is considered the group's most important effort. Its hook-filled hip-hop beat is the perfect background for the "tale of terror" of shopping for clothes . . . with your mother! Every teen can relate to that particular ordeal, and Will's clever lyrics brought it all home with a laugh.

And if the words alone didn't do it, the video certainly did. As wacky as the song, the freewheeling "Parents Just Don't Understand" video hip-hopped its way onto MTV and flipped into heavy rotation.

Whatever the rhythm 'n' rhyming subject—their parents, themselves, dating, or horror movies—the songs and the videos from *He's the DJ, I'm the Rapper* struck a chord with listeners. The album exploded onto the charts and quickly racked up sales. Within a matter of months, it had sold over three million copies. In fact, *He's the DJ, I'm the Rapper* helped Will and Jeff do exactly what they'd set out to. They created their own special niche in the world of rap and set themselves up as "kings" of the genre, squarely in the limelight.

The kings got their share of slings and arrows aimed their way, courtesy, mostly, of hard-core hip-hoppers who loudly and publicly dissed Will and Jeff's music, labeling them "fakes" and "nerds." At first, Will was able to shrug some of it off. "I don't understand groups who come on stage looking real mad," he'd respond. "We just want people to have fun."

But as the sales snowballed, the limelight intensified and so did the criticism. To some in the rap community, what that frothy "Parents" had done was not so much crown Will and Jeff kings, but open the door of rap music to a more mainstream—read: white—audience. And those who considered themselves the founders, and protectors, of the genre didn't like it. They said Will and Jeff had sold out the core of hip-hop ideals. Their lyrics were dismissed as "suburban rap," completely contrary to the socially conscious messages of other rappers. Because Will and Jeff's songs

weren't about violence, drugs, life on the street
(which, after all, neither had experience with), they
were accused of not being authentic, of diluting an
art form, pandering to the mainstream audience
just to make a buck. The rapper Big Daddy Kane
insisted he was expressing the opinions of many
when he blasted Will and Jeff for making music for
white people, people who couldn't possibly understand the roots of rap.

Will and Jeff were stung. Who wouldn't be? But
they were far from chastised. The chart-breaking
duo wasn't about to cave to the demands of others,
no matter who they were. It wasn't just because
Will and Jeff were successful doing what they were
doing, it was because no matter what anyone else
said, *they* believed in what they were doing. The
songs they wrote and performed might not have
reflected the experience of others, but the music
was true to their own lives. And that had value.

And so the "war of words" began.

In an interview given to *USA Today,* Will and Jeff
addressed the issue of race in rap. "I don't think
anyone can dictate what's black and what's not
black. Big Daddy Kane is ignorant and doesn't
realize what black really means. He thinks being
articulate is being white. We're trying to show the
world, and black kids, that you can dress nicely and
speak well and still be considered black. Our music
is black music. Our families are black, we came
from black backgrounds." Will conceded, of
course, that he and Jeff didn't write street-themed
lyrics—if they did, then they'd first have to cop to
the "phony" label.

"We're going to continue to rap about things we *have* experienced," Will announced. "Not only that, lots of people can relate to us. In 'Parents Just Don't Understand,' we wanted to write about something everybody could relate to. I wasn't trying to appeal to a white audience, or do anything different. I was writing about what I related to, what I thought was interesting. It's from my own experience."

Will further explained that their appeal had nothing to do with color. It crossed all lines—rich or poor, black or white, prep school–acquired knowledge or street smarts. "We do rap from a different point of view. We make it fun. We make it universal. My point of view isn't limited. It's very broad. It's more than the black experience."

They were also slammed for their humor. Will and Jeff responded, "We *are* humorous, we like to have fun. We let our personalities run through our work. Both of us have a good sense of humor and we don't act any differently when we make a record. You don't have to come on rough to rap. If there's funny stuff on our album, it comes from us."

Will had a furious comeback for those who dissed them for not using profanity in their songs. "I would never do anything that my mother couldn't turn on her radio and listen to," he said defiantly. "I would never do anything to offend my family."

And don't think Caroline Smith didn't appreciate that. The woman who'd been dead set against Will's rap career became his staunchest supporter.

"This album's good, even I can stand to listen to it," she said, giving her thumbs-up to the effort.

In the end Will challenged his detractors with a question. "Why do you have to compare DJ Jazzy Jeff and the Fresh Prince with other rappers? Rap is just like any other kind of music. You can't compare Luther Vandross to Michael Jackson, so why do we have to be compared to Public Enemy or Tone-Loc? All rap is real."

Whether Will's arguments ever did sway his detractors is questionable. But they say that living well is the best revenge; Will and Jeff got that, big time, starting with recognition and awards. In January 1989 DJ Jazzy Jeff and the Fresh Prince swept the Rap category at the annual American Music Awards. They took home statuettes for "Best Album" and "Best Artist."

A month later the duo made rap history by winning the first ever Grammy Award for Rap as "Parents Just Don't Understand" snagged the vote for "Best Rap Single."

Once again, their victory was accompanied by criticism. The recognition by the mainstream music industry just added fuel to the fire. Those members of the rap community who wore their "outsider" status as a badge of honor used the Grammy win as just another example of Will and Jeff "selling out."

That wasn't the reason, however, that Will and Jeff didn't show up to accept their award. In a move that stunned the music industry, the pair actually boycotted the ceremony. Though the stodgy Grammy committee had finally created a rap category, they apparently didn't feel the award had enough merit to be given out at the televised ceremony. The rap award, in fact, was lumped in with the technical awards and others considered of less interest to mainstream audiences. Therefore, it was handed out at a nontelevised event.

If they couldn't be on the show, Will and Jeff decided to be no-shows. They weren't just grandstanding, but standing up for what they believed in. "It's like going to school for twelve years and then not being able to walk across the stage [and get your diploma]," they groused. They made their point: From that year on, the rap category was included as part of the big show.

In spite of all the accolades and applause coming their way, Will and Jeff managed to maintain a fairly objective attitude about their place in rap history. They realized that *some* of their success, at least, had to do with being in the right place at the right time. "The bottom line is rap is generating the most money of any form of music right now," Will observed in an interview. "The music is good. It's realistic. It's here. Mainstream businessmen and the industry are opening up."

Though Will may have been able to keep an even perspective on his musical success, with that success came money. Lots of money. More money than he had ever seen before. And he wasn't able to keep any sort of a sane perspective on that.

Will and Jeff began to spend that money as fast as they made it. The duo hired an entire posse of bodyguards, roadies, and dancers to accompany them wherever they traveled. They were less than discriminating employers. In fact, the only qualification necessary to be a member of the posse was to simply be one of Will and Jeff's friends from the old days back in Philly.

The pair rode around in limousines and went to the priciest restaurants. They attended parties and Hollywood events where they met and chilled with the movers and shakers of the industry, including Eddie Murphy, Will's childhood idol.

Will's entire posse went on tour to promote the worldwide release of *He's the DJ, I'm the Rapper.* They experienced "livin' large" all over Europe, Russia, and Japan. And while Will and the guys were tasting borscht and sushi for the first time, the cash register back home was ringing up more and more sales. It wasn't only the music that was selling. DJ Jazzy Jeff and the Fresh Prince started their own 900 number info line—which soon turned into a 900 number info gold mine. The rappers simply prerecorded daily messages for their fans, who responded eagerly to the new venture. In the first six months the line was set up, it received over two million calls—at an average of $2.45 a pop. Record company executives were taking bets that Will and Jeff would make more money on the telephone than on the album itself.

When the time came to record their third album, Will and Jeff decided to do it right: and spend more money. "We have to record—why not go someplace exciting to do it?" was the thought. They headed off, posse in tow, to the Bahamian resort Compass Point. There they rented rock legend Robert Palmer's posh beachside villa. Will still marvels at the sight and sound of the waves that splashed right up against his window there.

Needless to say the entire entourage was impressed, and happy about the change in scenery, especially since the trip was *gratis* Will and Jeff. Of course, it wasn't all rest and relaxation. Some work got accomplished. After a dozen days in paradise, they did manage to complete four songs for the new album.

To be fair, Will and Jeff made a stab at keeping their priorities straight. They tried to remain humble. They called home every day when they were away and even sent for Mom and Dad to come along on some tour dates. In the press, Will quipped, "I'm pretty much the same person. Success hasn't changed me much. Now, the difference is, I can get two burgers instead of one."

If it had only been that simple. The fact is that success had already turned to excess, only they didn't see it that way. Will was a millionaire by his eighteenth birthday, and he continued to spend the money as quickly as he earned it. "One year I spent $800,000," he admits. "I went through it so fast, it made my head spin. Being able to buy anything you want makes you a little crazy."

Indeed, Will went a lot crazy.

He went on spending sprees that gave new meaning to the phrase "shop till you drop." He took trips on the spur of the moment and invited whoever was around to come along for the ride. He gambled, both in the casinos of Atlantic City and Las Vegas, and also in the confines of his home—a friendly $2,000 wager on a game of pool wasn't unusual. He bought cars, seven of them, to be exact. Included in Will's fleet was a Corvette, a candy-apple red Camaro, a truck, a Suzuki bike, and a Suburban Station Wagon with a 2,200-watt custom installed stereo system. As a matter of fact, one of the "basics" on every one of Will's vehicles was a very loud stereo system.

Jewelry was another big ticket item Will scooped up with abandon. Perhaps the most ostentatious was a gold necklace that spelled out "Fresh Prince" in diamonds. Of course, the necklace faded in the shadow of the mansion Will bought in Merion, a suburb of Philadelphia. He and his brother Harry camped out in luxury in that house. He installed a hot tub in the middle of the bedroom, a pool room in the foyer, a basketball hoop as the centerpiece of the living room. His kitchen was described as "looking like a mini-mart with rows of bottled juice in the cabinets and dozens of cuts of meat in the freezer."

Naturally, clothes took a big bite out of Will's "budget." His criteria for buying outfits was astonishingly simple: If it caught his eye, he walked out of the store with it. "Even if it was ugly, I bought it," Will recalls, chagrined. "Once I flew to London and Tokyo just to buy clothes." Another time, when he and his posse were in Atlanta, a call was put in to the Gucci store there. "Close it, we're coming," Will's people instructed the managers. They did—and were rewarded with mega sales for their cooperation. "It was a power trip," Will later said.

But there was one thing all of Will's money

couldn't buy. That was happiness. "I spent a long time trying to figure out how things could be going so well, and I could be so unhappy," he admitted.

Another thing Will could not buy was respect. While so many yes-people were fawning all over him, Will also came face-to-face with bigotry. He still recalls the embarrassment of settling into his first-class seat on a plane, only to be questioned by the flight attendant who demanded to see his ticket, sure that he couldn't possibly belong there. For neither Will's thick pocketbook nor his status as "king" of the rappers mattered a bit to those bigots who saw only a young black man with expensive clothes, cars, and jewelry. "In the two years I had my Corvette, I probably got stopped [by the police] thirty-five or forty times. At least five to ten of those times, I was told I was stopped because ' . . . we want to know where you got this car. . . .' A young black guy with a nice car is going to get stopped, period. And the cops will tell you that."

While Will was disgusted, he wasn't particularly surprised. His parents had taught him about life's realities, unfair as they were. Will has admitted, quietly, to some rough treatment by law enforcement officers, though he has never filed suit.

Will's fantasy and his reality were colliding. He had achieved the goals he thought he wanted and was rewarded well beyond his imagination. Yet deep down he wasn't happy. Deep down he knew he was messing up big time. "There was nothing funny about it," he says of those days. "It was a matter of being young, wild, and stupid. But there was nothing anyone could have done. At that age, with that amount of money, it's difficult to handle. And because I was eighteen, the checks came to me. So it was difficult for anyone to intervene in the ludicrous behavior I was displaying. Besides, I didn't listen to anyone. Everything my parents taught me was out the window as soon as that cash hit the bank account."

It wasn't as if Will's parents weren't trying to stop the insanity. His mom begged him to stop driving so fast so he wouldn't be stopped by the police, and to stay away from drugs. Will's father was just plain disgusted. "He saw me blowing money that could allow me to set myself up for the rest of my life."

But if Will didn't listen to his folks, there was another entity he had to obey: the IRS. And one day he got a wake-up call courtesy of the tax man. He owed the government millions. For not a cent of Will's earnings had been put away to cover his income taxes. Looking back on the day he got that shocking news, Will says, "There's nothing more sobering than having six cars and a mansion one day, and you can't even buy gas for the cars the next."

It hadn't really taken very long—a mere ten months of free spending—to go broke. But even that wasn't the worst of it. For along with the reality check from the government, Will had to swallow another bitter pill. All those friends, the buds, the posse who were there for the good times and helped him spend the money went out-the-back-Jack when Will received his tax bill.

Being broke and semi-abandoned was a bummer, but Will felt worst about his situation for another reason. He knew he'd gone against the principles he'd been taught as a child. He was determined to get back to where he once belonged, to the values he once believed in. Will sums it up: "I had a period in my life where I sought attention, had a little money, and wanted to flex it all. But the real person inside me eventually dictated how I had to act, how I had to behave, and how I had to treat people. My parents and my upbringing weighed out over the temptation of the glitter, the money, and all that. Who I really am wins every time."

As it turned out, Will's luck was about to change, thanks in part, at least, to "who he really was."

Chapter **4**

Bustin' Fresh

The year 1990 marked not only the dawn of a new decade, but as it would turn out, the sun rising on the fortunes of a wiser and more directed Will Smith. As the calendar page turned to January, Will turned around to take stock of just how far he'd come, how far he'd fallen, and where he wanted to go from there.

He'd earned well over a million dollars before his twenty-first birthday, and managed to lose it all within that same year. "I was stone broke," Will admitted. He couldn't look to sales of his newest record to recoup some of his lost fortune, for DJ Jazzy Jeff and the Fresh Prince's third CD, *And in This Corner,* did not exactly come out of the gate swinging. That was the album they'd gone to the

A Biography

Bahamas to record. It didn't flop . . . exactly. It ended up with respectable sales, but it was far from a worthy successor to *I'm the DJ, He's the Rapper*. Did it signal that DJ Jazzy Jeff and the Fresh Prince were a flash in the rap pan? Perhaps that's exaggerating the situation, but Will was bummed about it nevertheless. "In 1990," he's said, "I was dealing with a decline in my music—at least in my eyes. I was looking for something new, something else to do." He didn't exactly say he wanted that next step to take place on screen, but the idea of becoming an actor had been percolating in Will's active mind for a long time.

As fate would have it, Will wasn't the only one searching for something that winter. Will couldn't have known it at the time, but a man he'd never heard of was looking for something, too.

The man was Benny Medina, a thirty-one-year-old African American, also making his mark in the music industry, but on the business side. At the time Benny was vice president in charge of the Black Music division at Warner Bros. Records, a position of power and respect, and a long way from his origins.

Benny Medina had grown up poor in the tough Watts section of East L.A. Besides the daily encounters with street violence, Benny had to deal with the worst thing that could happen to a fatherless child—his mother died and there were no relatives to take him in. He spent much of his childhood "in the system," being shuffled in and out of foster homes and juvenile centers. When Benny was about to turn fifteen, he was sent to live with another foster family in a whole new part of town: the posh Beverly Hills.

The home belonged to movie and TV composer Jack Elliot, his wife, and their three children. Mr. Elliot was a member of the Hollywood elite. His friends included such showbiz legends as Frank Sinatra, Dean Martin, and even Motown Records founder Berry Gordy. How could street-kid Benny possibly adapt to such a situation? Better than anyone might have guessed. In fact, as he would later quip, "I literally put on a backpack and rode my bike to their home in Beverly Hills. I never left."

Benny moved into the garage, which had been converted into living quarters. "My deal was that I had to maintain good grades, keep a job, and respect the household," he explained. "I was kind of an aggressive, smart-ass kid coming into a place where they had such a completely different background. I could never figure out how I was going to exist in that household."

Exist he did, and more. At the Elliots, Benny received the kind of love and discipline he had never experienced before. In spite of the culture clash, things went so well that the Elliots ended up adopting Benny. They gave him a home, a family, and opportunities he never dreamed of before. It was something out of a storybook . . . well, maybe not exactly, but as Benny began making his own mark in the music world, an idea started to grow. He realized his own rags-to-riches story might make a great TV series. He became obsessed with the idea.

And as with many a good idea, it took an accident to set it in motion.

Benny had never met Will but, being in the music business, was certainly familiar with the "Parents Just Don't Understand" video. Later, he'd recall thinking that Will was a natural comedian. For his part, Will had never heard of Benny Medina. But when they crossed paths at a special taping of *The Arsenio Hall Show* (which just so happened to be a tribute to multitalented musician and producer Quincy Jones), their lives collided and were forever altered. In fact, the two didn't exactly meet at the taping, but outside, in the parking lot. That was when the rapper asked for directions to his next destination, an L.A. Lakers basketball game. Benny recognized Will as the rapping half of DJ Jazzy Jeff and the Fresh Prince. They chatted for a while, and in the conversation Will mentioned he wanted to try his hand at something new—maybe acting.

That's when it clicked. Benny replied that he, in fact, *had* an idea for a TV series. A sitcom based on his own life story, it might be just the right thing for Will.

They left it at that for the moment, and Will headed for the Lakers game, which he almost missed! "Benny gave me terrible directions," Will would laugh when he recounted their first meeting. To which Benny would counter, "If he wanted directions, he asked the wrong guy. But if he wanted someone to get him on TV, he came to the right guy."

Indeed. With a possible "star" for his show in

mind, Benny next went after a producer. He approached Quincy Jones with the idea, who instantly warmed to the concept. Quincy also knew exactly which TV network to pitch it to. NBC, long the network king of comedy on Monday nights, was on the lookout for a hot new sitcom. One of its major hits was *ALF,* a comedy about a silly, smart-mouthed, but lovable alien. By 1990, however, *ALF* was on its last ratings legs. "We were looking for a replacement for *ALF* on Monday at 8 P.M.," admitted an NBC programming executive. "A show we thought would have kid and teen appeal as well as being a family show." Clearly, NBC was the network with a "hole" to fill. Benny and Quincy knew just how to fill it.

To prepare the executives, Quincy first sent over some tapes of Will on *Yo! MTV Raps* for (then) NBC Entertainment head Brandon Tartikoff, and network chief Warren Littlefield. Then Benny and Quincy went for their pitch meeting. They outlined their idea for the series, and Benny explained his background. "Hmmm, cute life," Tartikoff casually commented as he showed them out. But the next day a deal with NBC was made. What was once just an idea steamrolled into the reality of *The Fresh Prince of Bel Air.*

But first things first . . . the idea was sold, but the inexperienced Will still had to prove he could carry a TV series. In early 1990 Quincy invited the NBC brass out to his Bel Air home to see Will audition. Script in hand, Will disappeared into a bedroom to rehearse. It was a nerve-racking moment. Everyone there wanted Will to succeed—but for various reasons. The network execs saw Will's popularity as a rapper translating into mega-ratings for them; Quincy and Benny saw an idea they'd nurtured about to come true; Will saw his dreams of taking that next step as an entertainer at his fingertips.

When Will emerged from the bedroom, he was far from cool. "There were beads of sweat," Warren Littlefield recalled. "But Will read from a script and just nailed it. I sat there thinking, 'Whoa! Just bottle this guy!'"

Benny also remembers, "Will put some of his personal nuances in, and right after that, everybody was shaking hands, hugging and kissing."

All that was left was to sit down and hammer out the exact details of the show. Though Benny's life would be the basis for the series, there were some changes made right away. Benny recalled that when he first moved in with the Elliots, there was an African American family who lived nearby. "That family freaked me out," he says. "There was no relationship between what *I* considered to be the black experience and what *they* considered the black existence in America. It was like two completely different cultures." That clash could be both dramatic and funny at the same time, so Fresh Prince's rich family went from white to black. And instead of the "Prince" being a foster child, he became a cousin from back East who'd been getting into trouble and got shipped off to live with his rich relatives. The idea was, both sides had a lot to learn from each other.

To kick off the series, NBC hired Andy and Susan Borowitz, a husband/wife sitcom writing team, whose credits included such hits as *Family Ties, Square Pegs,* and *Archie Bunker's Place.* They knew the ins and outs of sitcoms, but admittedly didn't have a clue about rap, or Will's appeal through that medium. After a three-week "crash course" spent watching videos and listening to rap CDs, augmented with lessons from Will on the difference between "fly" and "def," they were off and running. "It was a whirlwind thing," recalls Susan Borowitz.

Together, the writers created the characters of Aunt Viv and Uncle Phil Banks, and set up the concept. Using his own personality for his TV alter ego, Will created a character—also named Will Smith—all of America could come to love. He described the character as "innocent, silly, fun-loving, bound for trouble," and even incorporated his real-life rap background into the situation. The TV Will did not perform, but like most black teens he knew, he loved the beat from a boom box. The comedy, of course, grew out of the culture clash Benny Medina saw all those years ago. The play on words as well as on attitudes led to snappy dialogue. In one early scene Will's aunt and uncle made plans for his education. Aunt Vivian said, "Will will go to Bel Air Academy." Uncle Phil offered, "Good for you. I used to fence at Bel Air." To which the streetwise Will, pointing to their CD player, rejoined, "Really? How much you think we could get for that stereo?"

Will's TV family comprised talented, experienced actors. James Avery, who played Uncle Phillip Banks, had appeared in numerous TV series *(L.A. Law, St. Elsewhere, Beauty and the Beast)* and feature films *(Fletch, License to Drive, 8 Million Ways to Die)*. The original Aunt Vivian Banks, Janet Hubert-Whitten, had performed on Broadway, in TV series, and in movies. Karyn Parsons, who was cast as the Valley girl cousin Hilary Banks, had been acting since the age of thirteen with various commercials and TV series appearances on her resume. Alfonso Ribeiro was cast as the "stuffed shirt" cousin Carlton Banks; he had starred on Broadway in the *Tap Dance Kid* when he was twelve years old and had co-starred in the TV series *Silver Spoons*. Two-time *Star Search* winner, Tatyana M. Ali, all of twelve at the time, portrayed youngest cousin Ashley Banks; she got her start at six years old when she appeared as a regular on *Sesame Street,* and then guested on *The Cosby Show, Hawk,* and *All My Children.* Finally there was Joseph Marcell, a respected, classically trained British actor who was making his American TV debut as Geoffrey the butler. All in all, *The Fresh Prince of Bel Air* boasted a pretty impressive group of actors. Except for one, that is.

Will walked onto the *Fresh Prince* set as a "baby" actor. But like any child, he was excited at the prospect of something new. His dream of getting a chance to act was coming true. Not only that, he'd be taking centerstage, the place he was always most comfortable in. And, no small matter, with his *Fresh* paycheck he was going to be able to settle his debt with the IRS.

But Will's excitement was based on more than that. The more reflective Will cared less about his own rising star than what good he might do. "What I am happiest about is that I can be a role model and give people something to think about," he said. "It's important to have a black show that's positive. Television has been controlled by white America and they've had a tendency to put their own on."

Clearly, from the get-go Will took his TV mission seriously. The natural confidence that allowed him to believe "I can do anything!" was still there, albeit tempered a bit by the mistakes he'd made in the previous two years. He read the scripts over and over and would point out when something—dialogue, a motive—wasn't coming off as he thought it should. Will questioned it all. He wanted everything to be perfect.

The truth is, this new adventure was putting a lot of pressure on Will. He didn't want to fall flat on his face and be embarrassed, particularly in front of his homeboys back in Philly. Some of them were wary of the whole deal. "There was kind of a concern about the unknown," Will says. "I was one of the first of the hip-hop generation on television, so there was a sense of wonder if it was going to translate, about how America would accept this hip-hoppin', be-boppin', fast-talking kind of black guy."

The confident side of Will felt "I have a pretty good eye and ear for what America will think is funny." But the once-burned part of Will admitted that he was taking a big chance, acknowledging that "this is the only acting I have ever done."

Clearly, Will was hardly blind to his lack of

acting experience. And in his own eyes, it showed. He felt he was just plain bad—bad as in really bad, that is, not bad as in good. After he saw the pilot of *Fresh Prince,* Will confessed to his friends, "There were things I could have done better. I missed the rhythm, I didn't quite hit the laughs."

He needn't have been so hard on himself. The pilot, aired first for a private preview audience, ended up being NBC's highest-testing comedy series—it even got higher marks than *Cosby* had in its first preview. It was predicted that Will would be a "big, breakout star." Brandon Tartikoff began describing Will as the "next Eddie Murphy."

When the show debuted in September 1990 for a mass audience, the reviews reflected the test audience's reaction. They were a lot more positive than Will's private assessment of himself. Though some reviewers called the show itself "air-headed" and "silly," almost all praised Will for his "natural acting ability." A critic for *The New York Times* wrote: "One initial doubt about the program has already been resolved, however: Mr. Smith not only can sing, write, and dance, he clearly can act, too." Even when Will muffed a line, the *Times* writer thought he was terrific: "[Will] called out, 'Sorry, Mom,' to his mother, visiting from Philadelphia and watching the performance from the audience." *TV Guide*'s review read in part, "Will Smith's enjoyment of his role is infectious."

It wasn't just great reviews; the ratings were solid, too. When *The Fresh Prince of Bel Air* beamed out over the TV screens of America, audiences gave it a rousing thumbs-up. The show was up against CBS's comedy *Uncle Buck* and ABC's action series *MacGyver,* and initially, at least, it handily outpaced the competition. As the weeks went by, however, *Fresh Prince* and *Uncle Buck* seesawed back and forth for the title of time-slot king. But that just reinforced Will's resolve. He'd always loved the challenge of competition, rapping on a street corner, or here in Hollywood. "I'm going to fight back," he declared. "I'm going to make sure [*Uncle Buck*] never wins again!"

And in the end that's exactly what happened. The CBS show began to falter and was eventually canceled. While ABC's *MacGyver* stayed on the air, it was *The Fresh Prince of Bel Air* (later coupled with *Blossom*) that put NBC right back on top.

The phrase "Must-See TV" hadn't been coined yet, but for America's youth, Will Smith became their must-be new idol. They soon imitated everything Will—his attitude, his expressions, even his sartorial style. The loud, colorful skids and mismatched, laceless Air Jordans, his backward baseball cap, sports-team jerseys, and baggy jeans were must-have outfits because Will Smith wore them. By 1991 there wasn't anyone who didn't understand: The erstwhile rapper had turned himself into a genuine TV icon.

Chapter 5

Welcome to "Hollyweird"

The *Fresh Prince of Bel Air* was the best thing that could have happened to Will Smith at that time in his life. But it didn't come without a downside. And that downside was not unanticipated, at least not by Will. For as the season progressed, it became clearer and clearer to Will that he was in way over his head as an actor. He was his own worst critic. "I sucked. Badly," Will assessed of his acting on the first *Fresh Prince* episodes. "I can't believe how many mistakes I made."

Worse, no one took him seriously when he expressed his doubts. "I was wondering at the beginning why no one ever asked if I could act," he recalled. "Not Quincy, not NBC. Nobody. They

51

even shot the pilot and never asked me, 'Can you act?'"

Only Will's persistence, charm and willingness to accept responsibility for his mistakes—and learn from them—kept him from drowning. Will only hoped he could tread water long enough to learn this new craft.

There was a lot to learn. In the very beginning his voice didn't carry, he missed his floor marks, and director Debbie Allen needed to prod and cajole a more animated performance out of him.

Will cringes as he remembers, "I was trying so hard. I would memorize the entire script, then I'd be mouthing everybody's lines right back at them—while they were talking. When I watch those episodes, it's disgusting. My performances were horrible." It was toughest on his co-stars, because he often threw them completely off balance. Tatyana Ali, who was much younger than Will, but much more experienced, revealed recently, "I couldn't believe what a bad actor he was. I'd do a scene with him and he would mouth my words while I was doing my lines . . . If you look at the old shows, you can see it." Will now admits he did it out of fear—plain old unmitigated terror. "I was afraid of missing my lines," he explains.

What made it even harder was the fact that while Will was stumbling along in front of the cameras, off camera, the Hollywood hype machine was in overload. Important people, those who were supposed to be "in the know," were saying all these amazing things about Will—and he knew he wasn't even measuring up.

NBC head honcho Brandon Tartikoff kept describing Will as "the next Eddie Murphy" and
"The Great Rap Hope." "Will has this very infectious personality, with a great spirit," he'd an-
nounce. "What he has, you can't teach. I think the
Eddie Murphy comparison is there."

Will's friend and mentor Quincy Jones added
fuel to the fire when he told *TV Guide* in a 1990
interview: "I know real stars. I've worked with
Streisand, Sinatra, Michael Jackson. Will Smith
has the same potential to climb to the same heights
as those greats. He's a monster talent."

Add to that the whirlwind of publicity NBC had
Will doing—photo shoots, interviews, press con-
ferences, promotional trips; the pressure was overwhelming. That first season Will appeared on *The
Tonight Show* an amazing four times.

Another novice might have collapsed under the
weight of the hype and expectations. Someone else
may have started believing the glowing press reports. But not Will Smith. He'd already been
through one top-of-the-heap to bottom-of-the-
barrel experience, and if nothing else, he'd learned
his lesson. To Will's credit, he did not buy into the
massive ego stroking. Instead, he tried to deflect
the barrage of overwhelming and overinflated
praise.

Ironically, Will came from the world of rap
where boasting and bragging in rhyme was an art
form. And Will was a master of hip-hop hype. But
that was something else; Will knew the praise he
was getting for *Fresh Prince* was really undeserved.
That's why it made him very uncomfortable.

Will actually confronted Brandon Tartikoff about the quotes he was reading everywhere. "Don't compare me to Eddie Murphy," he told his boss. "That's putting a lot on my shoulders." The network executive protested, "Will, it's out of love. I was there when Eddie was nineteen. I saw what he did with his career and talent, and I see the exact same thing in you."

When reporters repeated such quotes, Will tried to be clear about his discomfort. "People are expecting a lot, and I've never done any acting, so I don't want to be compared to anyone. I have a natural feel, but let me practice first so I can be proud of what I do."

At times Will felt like he was thrown into the water without a life preserver. Not only did he have to learn a whole new craft, but he had to *unlearn* much of what he had been doing very successfully, as Will explained to a reporter. "This is really new for me. I had to learn not to look at the camera. In videos, that's what you do."

When Will made those admissions, it wasn't because he was suddenly "Mr. Humility." He was really asking for help with his acting. Only he never got it. Instead, he got excuses made on his behalf by the very people who should have been working with him to develop his natural talent.

The producers, Andy and Susan Borowitz, would sidestep the issue and answer queries about Will's acting with "We are seeing improvement every day. Will has natural ability. It's not like we pulled some schmo off the street."

Quincy Jones was of little help. He told Will that

Will turns his natural charm on for the cameras. (Bernhard Kuhmstedt/Retna)

With his musical partner, Jeff Townes, aka DeeJay Jazzy Jeff, Will cut five hot rap CDs and won three Grammy Awards.

Karyn Parsons played ditzy cousin Hilary Banks in *The Fresh Prince of Bel Air*—off camera, the two were great friends.

(Greg De Guire/ Celebrity Photo)

"Peace," Will's greeting to his legion of fans.

Doing a scene with James Avery, who played Uncle Phil on *The Fresh Prince of Bel Air,* Will used to be so nervous he'd mouth the lines of the other actors while they were saying them! (Chris Mackie)

Dressing sharply and piling on the jewelry was a hallmark of DeeJay Jazzy Jeff & The Fresh Prince.

(Janet Macoska)

Will and his steady, Jada Pinkett, made a "Trey sandwich" as the happy threesome donned combat fatigues for the premiere of *ID4*.

(Steve Granitz/ Retna)

Making the jump from rap star to TV star to action-movie megastar makes Will Smith one happy performer.

(Kathy Hutchins)

Will took home a trophy at the Blockbuster Video Awards for his movie *Bad Boys.*

(Steve Granitz/Retna)

Will and Linda Fiorentino film a scene from *Men in Black* at Battery Park in New York City.

(Bill Davila/Retna)

Will holds hands with the two most important women in his life—Jada and his mom, Caroline—at a Hollywood movie premiere.

(Kathy Hutchins)

"**A** hole in one" is how Will feels about his life right now—everything's just about perfect. An avid golfer, he can play on his own private course next to his house.

(F. de Lafosse/Regards/Retna)

he didn't need acting lessons. Like everyone else, Quincy told Will "just do what I'm doing. He told me that if a blind man is walking in the right direction, you don't stop him." Of course, Will might have added, when the blind man starts *bumping* into things, a little *assist* might be required!

Will turned to his co-stars for help, but he didn't get it there, either. Even they were intimidated by his hype. If his castmates wanted to make suggestions, they were hesitant—after all, Will was handpicked by the network brass and was being touted as "the next Eddie Murphy."

It would take a year until Will was finally able to vent his frustration to his co-stars. James Avery recalls the day his TV nephew finally said what was on his mind. "After that first year," James remembers, "Will said to us, 'I'm really mad at you people. You let me get out there on stage and make a fool of myself.'"

Those feelings, buried or open, didn't make for a totally comfortable set. Will respected his co-stars and knew they were talented. "The only thing that saved me on the show that first year was that everybody *else* in the cast was funny," he has since admitted. He eventually came to understand that his overnight success might not have been so easy for them to accept. After all, they had put in years of hard work to get where they were, and suddenly he was a star!

Tatyana Ali can now reveal that she and Will did not exactly bond at first. It wasn't just her lack of respect for his acting abilities—she didn't get along with him personally, either. "I liked his rap music, because he was the only rapper my mother let me listen to, but at first we weren't pals."

Will agrees, recalling, "That first year Tatyana and I clashed because I felt like her older brother and she wasn't having any of it."

There were other discordant voices in the mix, too. They came from Will's old rap world. Groups like 2 Live Crew and Public Enemy were making headlines over their controversial lyrics at the time. They stood accused of encouraging black youth to turn to violence to get what they wanted. Mainstream TV critics, who hadn't bothered to differentiate between what Will did as a rapper with the hard-core hip-hoppers, began to question whether Will's rap roots were such a good thing after all for prime-time TV.

At the same time Will was once again being slammed by old foes in the hip-hop community for being a fake and a sellout. Fab 5 Freddy, one of the hosts of *Yo! MTV Raps,* loudly dissed Will *and* his TV series for taking a "soft, *Cosby*-like approach to black youth culture."

Benny Medina and Quincy Jones took that criticism head on, proclaiming that *Fresh Prince* wasn't soft at all, but the same kind of groundbreaking TV that *All in the Family* had been years before. Will, stung by negative comments from his peers, still answered them thoughtfully. "I have a lot of opinions. I agree with things that Chuck D and Public Enemy say, but I have a different way of expressing myself. I like blending a message with comedy so it's subtle. I want people to enjoy themselves, then be left with something subliminally." It didn't exactly put an end to the sniping, but having expressed himself, Will let it go at that.

Between his own insecurities and the swirl of controversy going on around him, life—while on the whole, good—wasn't easy for Will Smith. He had something else to deal with, too: his new life in Hollywood. The Philly boy had moved not into a Beverly Hills mansion, but a modest apartment in Burbank near the NBC studios. Though far from lavish, he did furnish it with "totally Will" necessities: a mini–pool table in the living room, TVs and VCRs, plus his ever-expanding Nintendo collection. Will was very big into video games then, and at one time had forty-three cartridges strewn about the living room.

Will actually found a great deal of solace spending hours at home, either alone or with friends, playing video games, listening to music, or watching tapes on his VCR. It didn't hasten the assimilation process, however. Just as his TV character encountered East Coast/West Coast culture shock, so did Will. Only this was real life. "It's different here," Will claimed. "I'm an in-the-house type of person. I'm not out at the clubs and anything like that. I just don't hang out with too many new people."

However, unless you *are* out-and-about in L.A., you *don't* meet new people. It's a very social, very networking kind of town, a fact that made Will feel all the more displaced. He also believed there was a real difference in personal priorities between East Coast folk and West Coast wilders. "Money means too much out here," Will observed. "People are *real* on the East Coast."

Will was even weirded out by California's trendy restaurants. Take Spago for instance. The ultimate "in" eatery in L.A., celebrities and entertainment moguls flock to its tables to taste the latest culinary delights. "I'll never understand that," Will said with true awe. "What do you go there for? Avocado pizza? No way! You'll never catch the Fresh Prince eating an avocado pizza! I'd rather go to McDonald's."

Will eventually realized that to make it in L.A., he had to bring a little bit of Philly with him. But instead of the entourage he surrounded himself with when he first made it in the music biz, Will was a little more selective. And loyal. His partner in rhyme, Jazzy Jeff, had been with Will from the beginning, and if the fledgling actor had anything to do with it, nothing was going to change that. Will brought Jeff onto *Fresh Prince* and secured him a guest spot as a not-so-cunning con man. Jeff took to the role and he eventually was written into the show as a recurring character. That led to the standard bit of Uncle Phil literally throwing him— bodily—out the Bankses' front door.

But Jeff wasn't in L.A. just to keep Will company. They were also in the studio working on their fourth album, *Homebase*. That made for a hectic schedule. "I'm doing the show from nine to five,"

Will explained at the time. "And from six to midnight, I'm in the studio working on the album. But as long as I get my eight hours of sleep, I'm fine."

Of course, keeping workaholic hours like that, it was no wonder that Will wasn't interested in Spago-tasting or late-night partying. "I don't need a social life," he maintained. "I've got to work now, and I'll have a social life when I'm thirty. I'm not into the L.A. lifestyle anyway. It takes your mind off work." Clearly, Will had not forgotten the hard lessons learned over the past two years.

Though he might not have made the comparison at first, in many ways Will really was following the footsteps of his former idol, the person he was constantly being compared to: Eddie Murphy. The comedian was born and bred in the New York City suburbs, and even with his mega success from his comedy concerts, albums, and films, he had settled down not in "Hollyweird," but in New Jersey. By the time Will was well into his first season on *Fresh Prince,* Eddie had become a friend. So who better to turn to for advice? Will asked the funnyman how he handled all the hoopla in L.A. He'll never forget Eddie's answer. "He told me to beware of Hollywood. He said don't get caught up thinking this is real life. It's *NOT* real life."

As they say . . . a word to the wise. Will didn't let his newfound fame overwhelm him. He kept it cool, even as he continued to read gushing headlines and reports on how *Fresh Prince* was going to be the top show on TV by the end of the first season. Will's comment to that was "Nobody knows what a runaway hit is until the fans say it's a runaway hit."

In the meantime, Will wasn't waiting to exhale—he may have had a rough adjustment on and off the set, but as always, he was driven to be the best he could be. "My motivation is that I hate not being on top," he explained about why he was working himself so hard. "I get mad by being creative."

In fact, while he was still struggling with his acting, creative Will had already started setting new goals for himself. He wanted bigger and better things—not toys, or anything materialistic, but bigger and better roles. And though he admitted it to no one but himself at first, bigger and better screens to play those roles on.

Sometime between the first and second seasons of *Fresh Prince,* and despite his insecurities, Will made a decision: Film was going to be the next frontier to conquer. Just as he'd been the first rapper to move to a TV series, he wanted to be the first to hip-hop onto the big screen. That dream wasn't going to happen, however, because someone had beaten him to the punch. It bothered Will, too. Rappers Kid 'N Play, who Will felt were his rivals in rap, already had made it to the big screen with their movie *House Party.* At one point Will lamented, "No matter how good a movie I do, it will always be second."

Prophetic? Not!

Of course, that same year Will said very definitely, "I am a rapper. I will *always* be a rapper."

Not!

What Will *won't* ever be is clairvoyant. Maybe his crystal ball was a little cloudy back then, but if there was one thing Will *could* see clearly after all the ups and downs of the past few years it was this: At the end of the day, the real secret to success in Hollywood was the same as the real secret to success and fulfillment anywhere. Be true to yourself.

Chapter 6

Six Degrees
of Respect

As the months went by, Will's true desire to make a movie kept getting stronger. It wasn't that he suddenly felt he'd turned into a great actor—he knew *that* was still a long way off. But everywhere he looked, he saw others from his background making the transition to movies. He felt the same way he had upon hearing that first rap song: "They weren't doing anything I couldn't do."

Aside from Kid 'N Play, by 1992 there were other rappers who'd turned big-screen dreams into reality. Ice T had made his acting debut in *New Jack City,* a gritty look at inner-city cops; LL Cool J starred in *The Hard Way.* And both novice actors received good reviews for their on-screen efforts.

That wasn't a surprise to Will. "The characters

they play are from their everyday lives," Will explained of his fellow rappers' easy transition from concerts to movies. "I think the music and the culture of rap breed an aura of honesty and realism that people can relate to. That's why it translates to the screen well."

However, when it was Will's turn to make the big jump, he chose a role that had *nothing* to do with his hip-hop image or his TV persona. And because he was still well aware of his acting limitations, Will decided to start small. Instead of looking to parlay his TV success into big-screen stardom, he took a role in an independent, small-budget film called *Where the Day Takes You.*

Very much an ensemble piece, *Where the Day Takes You* was a dark drama about a group of street-smart homeless kids, struggling to survive on Hollywood Boulevard. Dermot Mulroney, Sean Astin, Balthazar Getty, Alyssa Milano, Ricki Lake, and Nancy McKeon were the young stars who portrayed the kids society didn't want and who were forced to create their own street family. Will played Manny, a disabled kid who was confined to a wheelchair.

For Will, the appeal of *Where the Day Takes You* was twofold. It was a huge departure from his hip-hop, jokester image. If he did his job well, casting directors might consider him for a wider range of movie roles. But there was a much less selfish reason Will was drawn to *Where the Day Takes You.* It was dramatic, socially relevant, and carried an important message. Will got it right away. "Just seeing how people ignore the homeless was an amazing lesson. I was in full makeup on Hollywood Boulevard, and people didn't know me. It was a revelation seeing how cold people can be." Unfortunately, it was a revelation not many people got to experience: The movie did not get wide distribution and soon ended up buried on video shelves. Still, *Where the Day Takes You* had given Will his first taste of cinematic freedom. He loved it—and it was just his first bite of the apple.

Partly because he'd received good reviews for the movie, but mostly because *The Fresh Prince of Bel Air* continued to be a ratings winner, Will soon began receiving piles of film scripts on his doorstep. It seemed as if the movie industry had finally woken up to Will. Excited by the interest, he was raring to go and in quick succession announced that he was going to make the sci-fi thriller *Biofeed*, and then the baseball tale *Scout*. If neither of those sound familiar, however, it's because neither one ever got made. The movie business, as Will was finding out, was often a whole lot more talk than action. Still, those minor setbacks could not stop this train. Will signed on instead to be part of the Whoopi Goldberg–Ted Danson starrer, *Made in America*.

Released in 1993, *Made in America* was a comedy about a young girl's search for her biological father. As Whoopi Goldberg's daughter, Nia Long played a proud African-American high school senior who discovered that her real father was the character played by Ted Danson. Not only is he white, but worse, he's a tacky car dealer best known for his cheesy TV commercials. Will played

Tea Cake Walters, Nia's longtime friend and classmate, who was haplessly and hopelessly in love with her. Throughout the movie, his main goal was to add the "boy" to "friend" in their relationship.

Clearly, Will was not the main event in this movie, either. But he was cool with his "fourth banana" status. Indeed, he felt *Made in America* was a major opportunity for him. First of all, he knew he needed more big-screen experience. "I'm still working on my acting skills," he told reporters. "I feel I've improved, but I'm still not ready to step out with my own feature."

And, perhaps more important, *Made in America* was a chance for Will to work with a superstar like Whoopi Goldberg. That experience turned out to be everything Will hoped it would—and more. "Working with Whoopi was really cool. I learned a lot, including how to behave between scenes."

One of those lessons was to tame his natural rambunctious behavior and remain down-to-earth and levelheaded. Because of *Fresh Prince,* Will had come into the film with a horde of fans. Soon *Made in America*'s San Francisco location shoot was overrun with Will's fans, all screaming, cheering, and straining to get a peek at their Prince. During breaks Will didn't run and hide from the crowds, but politely and graciously gave autographs and posed for photos. The fan hoopla surrounding Will was noted by many, including *Made in America*'s producers, Michael Douglas and Arnon Milchan. By the time *Made in America* wrapped, the producers collectively decided, "We have to find more work for this kid."

There were others who agreed with the producers. Audience approval was reflected in the box-office receipts, but it was the *critics* who really caused a stir about Will. The reviews were unanimous—Will was great, fresh, and funny. Some even said that in his supporting role, he practically stole the movie from veterans Whoopi and Ted. With all that support, Will finally felt that he was ready for the next cinematic step: a starring role.

Actually, that step, when it did come, turned into more of a leap. For the film Will set his sights on would not only be his first starring role—it would be a complete turnaround from any character he'd ever played, or anyone might expect him to play. "If you lined up one hundred films, this would be the last one that people would expect me to do," Will admitted at the time. But as soon as Will heard about the upcoming film *Six Degrees of Separation,* he knew he wanted a huge part in it. He also knew that if he did get the main role, "it will pretty much make or break my dramatic career." In fact, *Six Degrees of Separation* would turn out to be the biggest risk Will would ever take.

Based on an award-winning play by John Guare, *Six Degrees of Separation* is considered a modern-day classic. It is "reel life from real life," a story about an incident that occurred in New York in the mid-1980s. A nineteen-year-old African-American con man pulled a very unique scam twice, on two wealthy and socially prominent families. He researched his victims, then showed up on their doorsteps with a tale of woe: He said he was a classmate of their son's at Harvard University, and that his name was Paul Poitier—his own father was the respected actor Sidney Poitier. The young man was well-dressed but somewhat disheveled because, he said, he had just been mugged and had no money. He had the couple's address because their son had given it to him. Because they had no reason to disbelieve him, the wealthy parents invited this stranger into their home, giving him not only shelter and money, but their friendship.

It was *all* a lie. Sidney Poitier had no son. The con man was *not* a student at Harvard and did *not* know the sons of these two families. Not only did he take advantage of these people, but on one of his overnight stays, he slipped out after everyone was asleep and brought back a male visitor to their home. When the couple found the two of them together the next morning, they realized they had been dangerously deceived, that this "nice, young man" was not even close to what he seemed to be.

Deception was only part of *Six Degrees*. There were other themes as well, including racism: If the couple didn't invite Paul in, they'd appear to be racists. And to them, appearances were much more important than reality. *Six Degrees* also examined prejudice against homosexuality, another element of the Paul character. It tackled the theme of snobbery, too—these people believed Paul solely because he was dressed well and claimed celebrity connections.

The deeply serious themes of *Six Degrees* were about a zillion degrees away from anything Will had ever tackled before. *Fresh Prince* was light and joke-driven, as was anything Will had done in music. But that's exactly why Will was so excited about the prospect of being in this movie. "Showing you can do a complete 180 is what makes the movie industry stand up and pay attention," he knew, and doing it well in a leading role could be the stepping stone to blockbuster success. Will felt this role could be his major break as an actor and would make directors, producers, and the public look at him in a different way. "If I don't do a good job, it's a risk," he said. "This isn't a movie you'll take your kids to see. The biggest consideration for me was, if I pull this role off, I'm a legitimate actor. Hollywood doesn't really respect TV actors; film is the medium to succeed in. I want people to know there is something beyond what I can do in *Fresh Prince*. I want to be able to be accepted in any type of endeavor I choose."

Besides, even though Will used humor to deflect tough situations in his life, he still understood many of *Six Degrees'* themes all too well. Celebrity had not shielded him from the ugly taste of bigotry. "I meet people every day [to whom] I know I would just be another [expletive] if I didn't have a TV show," Will explained bluntly. "It's like, 'Well, I wouldn't let just any black guy into my house. But Will Smith, he's okay. He's a good black guy.'" Which, of course, precisely paralleled one of the themes of the movie.

Naturally, it was the central role of the cultured con man, Paul, that Will set his heart and soul on winning: It was the role of a lifetime.

Will wasn't naîve. He knew the odds were

against him because of his lack of experience, which would be all the more glaring alongside the stage-trained actors who'd already been cast, including Stockard Channing and Donald Sutherland. Another concern was Will's comic, hip-hop image—it was totally opposite of the character of Paul.

Still, Will truly believed, if he worked very hard, he could handle it. He also felt he had something unique he could bring to the part: His own real-life likability. "The audience has to accept that these people would let this guy into their house. I could sell that. It's something about my face or something that makes people accept me."

Even so, there was one concern Will did have that lingered about the role. *"Six Degrees* was the scariest choice I've ever had to make in my career," he confessed. "My big concern was for my rap career—you don't see too many rappers playing homosexual roles in films. The origins of the music are about masculinity, how tough you can be. So I was concerned about how my credibility would be affected."

But that worry was shelved, for the time being, when Will again realized success in *Six Degrees of Separation* could make the A-list of Hollywood's film elite stand up and notice him. "If I pull off something this dramatic," Will declared, "then Spike Lee and Steven Spielberg will want to work with me."

The truth is, it would take another three years for one of those two screen giants to work with Will, but in 1993 he did have certain things going for him. For one, the producers of *Six Degrees* just so happened to be the same guys who'd done *Made in America:* They didn't know if Will could pull off the role of Paul, but they *did* know he could draw an audience. And they were also very much swayed by Will's lobbying for the role. Both producer Arnon Milchan and director/screenwriter Fred Schepisi realized the young actor simply *wanted* the role of Paul more than any other actor they auditioned or even considered.

"Will showed up for our meeting in a three-piece suit and did a number on me, as they say," Mr. Schepisi recalls. "He did this with such incredible confidence and charm that the very act of his trying to convince me of his abilities did exactly that. He tried to convince me that he'd do whatever it would take, would go through whatever process, was sure he could get himself prepared. That confidence and charm was everything the character should be. He was worth taking a chance on."

In that meeting Will wasn't coming on like a know-it-all. He had confidence, all right, but he was also humble—he admitted straight out that he did not have a deep dramatic well of experience to draw on. That honesty impressed the writer, who said, "A lot of people think they can act, but they don't quite know the other level of experience that is required for a part of great magnitude. "In the end, what impressed me the most is that Will knew what he *didn't* know."

Something else Will probably didn't know was that *Six Degrees* may *not* have been made *without* him! Producer Milchan realized that Will's popularity and recognized name made him very bankable. And it was that "plus" that could possibly turn a noncommercial "art house" film into box-office success. A few weeks after his audition Will walked into the role.

Will kept his promise to do all he could to prepare for the toughest challenge of his career. It was an overwhelming undertaking, but as his dad had taught him so many years before, he tackled it "one brick at a time."

He made a mental list of what those "bricks" were: He had to change his voice and speech patterns to sound like a wealthy Harvard Ivy Leaguer. He had to change his physical presence for the role, and he had to understand exactly who this character was inside and out. And he had to do it all quickly. The director wanted all this accomplished before the first inch of film rolled through the camera. "Will has a reputation and a name, but this was a work of more substance," he said. "We weren't expecting to teach him about the whole acting experience, but we wanted him to have a healthy respect for what's involved."

So Will went to work. He flew to three cities to see different productions of the play and get a wide perspective on it. He hired a personal fitness trainer to get him into shape. He spent eighteen weeks with a dialect coach to nail Paul's speech patterns and cadences. And finally he got the acting coach he'd long suspected he needed. Still, it was tough, especially the first time he was handed a six-page monologue to memorize. "It almost made me not want to take the role," he now laughs. But once he got his rhythm, the challenge of all the hard work was exciting to Will.

He took it all seriously, but even in this most serious of situations, he couldn't completely stay in character. Translation: The set of *Six Degrees* was not without its lighter moments. A natural whirlwind of energy, Will brought a little bit of his TV background and a whole lot of himself to the situation. One insider tattles, "Early on in the filming, Will walked onto the set and let out this scream, which is the way he warms up on his TV show. The soundman practically jumped out of his seat as if his ears were being blown off."

Then there was the time Will and director Fred Schepisi were huddled together in a corner. Crew members tiptoed around. It had become a daily ritual for the two to discuss upcoming scenes: It was assumed that the veteran filmmaker shared words of wisdom and encouragement with the newcomer. Only this time Will broke the silence with a loud, "BAM!" and a fist-pump of excitement. All eyes turned just as Will jumped back to reveal an electronic chessboard and a boastful whoop of "I blocked your check, baby!" It broke the entire crew up.

But no one was laughing the day Will had to make a decision about a very touchy scene. The script called for Will's character to kiss the stranger he'd sneaked into the unsuspecting family's apartment. Just before the scene was to be shot, an uncomfortable Will told the director he couldn't do it. In the end they reworked the scene and shot it from a different angle: The effect was the same, but there was no real physical contact between the actors.

Later, Will felt worse about that decision than any other he'd made professionally. It showed he was still wet behind the ears when it came to being a committed actor. "It was very immature on my part," he said looking back. "I was thinking, 'How are my friends in Philly going to think about this?' I wasn't emotionally stable enough to artistically commit to that aspect of the film. In a movie with actors and a director of this caliber, for you to be the one bringing something cheesy to it, is disappointing. That was a valuable lesson for me. Either you do it or you don't." That was a lesson Will has never forgotten.

In spite of that one big regret, Will walked away from *Six Degrees* with more confidence and knowledge than he ever dreamed possible. And he came away with something else: Great reviews. *Newsweek* magazine asserted: "Smith, the rapper and star of TV's *Fresh Prince of Bel Air,* is an eye-opener in a complex, tricky part. Will Smith is going to be very big." *Time* magazine went with "As Paul, Will Smith is needy, daring, insinuating." *People* magazine decreed Will "remarkable" in his role of the con man. *Entertainment Weekly*'s reviewer praised: "Will Smith, in an impressive performance, makes [Paul] easy to watch—as smooth and transparent as glass."

The entire experience reinforced Will's original belief that *Six Degrees of Separation* had been the right move to make. "It was the best film experience I could have had. It has encouraged me to do more," he said.

But before Will could take the next step in his film career, he had another responsibility—to return to the next season of *The Fresh Prince of Bel Air*. It wasn't easy. As much as he loved doing *Fresh Prince*, to go from drama back to sitcom punch lines was jarring. "It took six shows to get back up to speed," Will admits. "I had to watch all the old episodes and go back to my old neighborhood in Philadelphia and hang with my buddies to get back into the mindset. To think: I was even starting to like [Paul's] khaki pants!"

Others recognized the problem, too. When Tatyana Ali had seen Will in *Six Degrees,* she "was completely blown away." It was obvious to her, her fellow castmates, and the powers-that-be on *Fresh Prince* that Will was developing into an accomplished actor. And strange as it may seem, that was cause for concern. Some of Will's bosses felt he might lose that natural touch he'd brought to *Fresh Prince*. They were less than thrilled, and Will sensed the tension. "The fact that I couldn't act was what made *Fresh Prince* popular," Will explained. "It was so real. People could connect with it. When I started the show, I was pretty much just playing myself, but now my life experience has gone beyond the life experience of the character. I'm finding myself having to act more now."

Ironically, the acting lessons he'd been discouraged from taking paid off—he took what he'd learned on *Six Degrees* back to the set of *Fresh Prince* and helped make the last several years of the sitcom its best ever.

Chapter 7

Growing Pains: All the Fun We Had—and Didn't Have!

Will returned to the set of *Fresh Prince* a different man with a new attitude. Perhaps no one quite realized it the first day of his return, but that new attitude signaled big changes for the show and the cast.

For a long time Will had been unhappy with the quality of the sitcom scripts. Not that the show wasn't funny—as a matter of fact, Will thought the slapstick humor was the *only* thing *Fresh Prince* had going for it. But that was the problem. Will couldn't squelch the feeling that *Fresh Prince* was, in fact, blowing an opportunity to say something really meaningful to its audience. He was determined to change that.

The "new and improved" Will expressed his opinion to the producers, the writers, and even the press. "I sense a great responsibility to make the show cutting edge, and I will no longer tolerate those things I disagree with," Will said firmly. "I really hate dumb jokes. I'm always fighting it. I keep saying, 'Why can't we be more like *Roseanne?'* That's the best show on TV. I'd love our jokes to have meaning beyond the superficial humor."

Additionally, Will pushed for the *Fresh Prince* scripts to more realistically reflect the world of young African Americans. He felt that a show as successful as *Fresh Prince* could carry a message that might potentially be heard by millions. And people just might listen to that message, precisely because it wasn't being hammered home with a heavy hand.

In an interview Will explained the direction he wanted to take *Fresh Prince.* "We're talking about a seventeen-year-old black man from the inner city and there are certain things he should be concerned with—sex and drugs, for two. He should have more involvement with friends from the inner city. There will be lots of touchy issues on the show, like prejudice. I want everyone to be enlightened when they watch our show. We're going to show Americans themselves!"

If Will thought his fresh opinions would be met with applause—or even acceptance—he was way off base. Just the opposite happened: Will's stance ruffled quite a few feathers. "In Hollywood there's a great resistance to change. I'm being met with much opposition," Will had to acknowledge. No one he met with—the producers, the network, nor the writers—were particularly keen on following Will's lead.

The *Fresh Prince* set had the ingredients for a major blowup. But just as the turmoil on the *Fresh Prince* set was threatening to erupt, someone stepped in and helped defuse the situation. It was, of all people, Bill Cosby, who had long been a hero to Will. The young actor had watched *The Cosby Show,* TV's highest-rated show at the time, with much interest. He'd observed how the relationships between the characters were woven together with laughter, love, and lessons. Will wanted to adopt that approach for *Fresh Prince.*

In a stroke of good timing Will bumped into Bill Cosby at a business party and poured his heart out to the old pro. He told Bill that he felt *Fresh Prince* was stagnating, not growing, and he asked the veteran funnyman's advice. He got it, too—but perhaps not exactly the way he envisioned it. Will remembers, "When I complained about the writing on the show, Bill suggested *I* write a script. 'Just write one and don't go to sleep until it's finished,' he told me." Will did and—lo and behold—learned a valuable lesson. Sheepishly he admitted, "When I met with the writers the next day, I had a lot less anger and a lot more understanding of the process."

That understanding was crucial, but it still didn't squelch his feelings that the show should tackle real issues. Will felt the *Fresh Prince* would be better, more responsible to its audience, if *he* could have more creative control. Needless to say, that attitude clashed—big time—with the show's producers, Susan and Andy Borowitz.

That disagreement opened up a sore that had been festering for some time. From the very beginning there were those—on and off the show—who questioned the Borowitzes' being the driving creative force of *Fresh Prince*. The self-proclaimed "yuppie" couple were not exactly in touch with the "Black Experience," whether it was from the inner city or the sunny suburbs. Perhaps Will had the deepest reservations about them, but until he felt more confident as an actor, he hadn't voiced his opinion. Now that he had spoken his piece, he expected changes to be made. They weren't. When Will felt the producers were turning deaf ears to his suggestions, he went over their heads. He asked for a meeting with Benny Medina and let it all out. Will's major concerns were twofold: The producers were more interested in the jokes than they were in the characters, and that they would not, and could not, address the interaction between blacks of different backgrounds.

Benny Medina agreed. The upshot was that Will would have more input in the storylines *before* they became scripts. Unfortunately, but not unsurprisingly, the producers were severely unthrilled with that decree. As Benny explained, "They decided, if that was the case, they'd rather not continue as producers—which none of us were upset about."

So it was out with the old and in with the new.

Winifred Hervey-Stallworth, a respected African-American TV show pro, was hired, and the change in the scripts was immediate. Will's character got a job and matured right before the audience's very eyes.

But that wasn't the *only* change. As Winifred worked more closely with Will and he was given more creative control, *Fresh Prince* showed new life and energy. The episodes were still funny and heartwarming, but more of them touched on meaningful subjects. Spirits were high on the set, and the cast really began to bond and become a tight-knit family. And, most important to the network, the *ratings* went up.

Fresh Prince went from being what the industry considered a "modest hit" to a solid gold success. In 1993, the first full season with Will's input saw *Fresh Prince* reach Number 14 for the year; Number 1 among African-American viewers, and the Number 1 8 P.M. sitcom during the all-important February sweeps month. *TV Guide* stated, *"The Fresh Prince of Bel Air* almost single-handedly kept NBC competitive on Monday nights."

Part of the ratings surge had to do with better quality scripts. As *Fresh Prince* reigned supreme in the ratings game, Will saw to it that all the episodes weren't just "joke-a-minute" exercises, but had some substance and meaning to them. One that Will is most proud of is the Christmas episode, which aired during the show's third season.

It was about how the true meaning of the holiday has slipped away from too many American homes. In the episode the Banks family decides to enjoy their holidays with a big family reunion at a Utah ski resort. It was picture perfect: a beautifully decorated tree, tons of presents under it, and the tantalizing aromas of tasty delights wafting from the kitchen. The relatives all were enjoying the Christmas spirit until the real world popped their beautiful bubble. The family was robbed at gunpoint, and the only thing left was a terrible feeling of being violated. As the horror of the moment seeped in, the Banks family had only each other to turn to for comfort. And in that they found the true meaning of the holiday.

"What I really like about this particular episode is having the family together," Will told a reporter who visited the set. "We have a great cast. I like what the audience receives from seeing the family together. The point of this episode is that there aren't any monetary gifts. They've all been stolen. The gifts have been removed, but the heart and the thought that originally went into the gifts is still there."

Perhaps one of the best "gifts" the entire cast received after that episode was a feeling of closeness with one another, something that had not always been there. *The Fresh Prince of Bel Air* had always been a polite, pleasant set, but even to the casual observer, the cast members seemed a bit standoffish with one another. All that changed during the third season.

Will had always been a barrel of laughs, and as the cast began to bond as a true family, they all got into the swing of being silly. Tatyana Ali's best memories are of the pranks they used to play on one another. She still gets the giggles recalling them. "There was this game we played," she described, "where you're eating something—like a sandwich or something. And, you know, when you're really enjoying your meal, when you get to the very last bite and you're really into your food? Well, somebody would always come up behind you and grab it out of your hand!"

Karyn Parsons, who played Hilary Banks, has similar recollections. "We had so much fun; we would laugh so hard that we would cry. All the time. But all of us were always—always—professional. We always got our job done. We had a successful show and we were laughing the whole way."

Things were so comfortable on the *Fresh Prince* set that the cast could laugh at Will's—and their own—mistakes. They decided to bring the entire audience watching at home in on the jokes by running their "blooper" reel over the credits at the end of each episode. *The Fresh Prince of Bel Air* was one of the first shows to start that tradition; many shows have since followed their lead.

Karyn remembers one particularly hysterical addition to the "blooper" clip: Will, who was off-stage, mooned James Avery in the middle of a scene. "James was supposed to look offstage and comment on something that was there," Karyn says with a laugh. "When he went to do it, Will's bare behind was, like, right in front of him! James couldn't hold it together! It was so hilarious. We put it on our 'blooper' reel. It was, like, 'Ayyyy, there's the biggest, hairy butt! Ayyyy!'"

But that was just the tip of the iceberg. When Will and his rap partner Jazzy Jeff got together, no one was safe. Not only did they share the same sense of humor, but Jeff was a constant reminder to Will of his roots: something Will never wanted to forget. Jeff's original guest spot turned into a regular gig; Will's loyalty to Jeff had remained strong.

The cast developed a tradition of gathering for a preshow huddle in Will's spacious dressing room before each taping, their smiles reflecting off the gold and platinum records that lined the dressing room walls. Everyone, regulars and that week's guest stars, would crank up the stereo and form a circle. One by one each actor would take the "center spotlight" position and dance or sing while the others clapped, whooped, and cheered, with cries of "Go, Will! Go, Karyn! Go, Alfonso!" The highlight of those preshow huddles had to be James Avery's weekly rendition of the "funky chicken." You had to be there.

Just before the actors were ready to bound onstage, each one would fling an arm into the middle of the circle until they were all touching hands. They'd whoop and yell and pump up their energy with shouts of "Focus! Focus! Love! Love!" And with a final cheer they'd bound out to the stage to tape the show in front of a lucky audience.

It was obvious that these actors loved being together—on and off the set. At one point Will had promised he would take the cast and crew to Hawaii for a vacation, and during the 1994 Thanksgiving holiday he did just that. Nineteen people from *Fresh Prince* chowed down on Maui's version of turkey and stuffing—all courtesy of Will.

The good vibes on the set continued to translate into great ratings for *Fresh Prince,* which kept getting renewed season after season. Before they knew it, the cast was taping their 100th episode. This milestone was celebrated with a crazy-mad party at the House of Blues club on L.A.'s Sunset Boulevard. Hundreds of friends and family joined the *Fresh Prince* posse as they partied throughout the night. An exuberant Will took a moment to talk to reporters and express his joy and gratitude at the show's success. "I want to do another hundred shows and make them as good as the first hundred!" he yelled above the happy hoopla. Then he thought for a moment and added, "And I'd love a film career."

Will was optimistic that he could, in fact, be a triple threat, able to juggle his recording, TV, and film careers. Alas, that turned out to be easier said than done. After trying to do it all, Will soon realized even he couldn't stretch in so many directions at once without snapping. In the end, it was his first love, music, that ended up on the back burner. "I have to wait until the show wraps before I can mentally set myself to do an album," Will explained. "And usually when the show wraps, I'm trying to get ready to do a film."

That said, Will and Jeff did come out with their fourth album, *Homebase,* during this time. They just couldn't support it with a major tour. "It's out of the question," Will had to tell both fans and the record company. But that didn't stop *Homebase* from hitting a home run. The single released from that album, "Summertime," actually won them a Grammy. Not too shabby. And not too accidental, either. Releasing "Summertime" was, in fact, a pretty crafty move. "The whole nation was in a dancing frenzy with songs from C&C Music Factory blasting the decibels in the clubs. Everything was hyper," Will recalls. "We just came out and slowed it all down, chilled it all out, by coming out with a groove record."

All told, things were going well. Too well, in fact. Just as Will was basking in the glory and good feelings that surrounded his multilayered career, he was hit smack in the face with a major problem: the "Aunt Viv" crisis. In spite of the real camaraderie that had developed among the cast members, it turned out that there *was* one sour apple. Actress Janet Hubert-Whitten, who played Aunt Viv, had tried to mask her unhappiness behind a smile, but she couldn't do it forever. She had become pregnant during the season, and although the pregnancy had been written into the show, still, there apparently were other unresolved issues. No one outside the *Fresh Prince* family really had a clue about Ms. Hubert-Whitten's unrest; in fact, many insiders knew nothing of it. All that changed during the course of the 1993 season when Ms. Hubert-Whitten was suddenly released from her contract. She remains the first and only original cast member to leave the show.

When that happened, the possibility of keeping it quiet dissolved. The press became involved, and the mudslinging began. Ms. Hubert-Whitten insisted there was a vendetta against her, but she had no idea why. She alluded to problems with Will and claimed that *he* got her fired. "Anyone who stands up to Mr. Smith on *Fresh Prince* is gone. Yes, I reprimanded him constantly for being rude to people and locking himself in his room, but I did not slander him in any way."

Will was impelled to respond. In a radio interview he countered that Ms. Hubert-Whitten brought a lot of personal baggage and problems to the set. The *Atlanta Journal* quoted Will: "I can say straight up that Janet wanted the show to be *The Aunt Viv of Bel Air Show*. She's been mad at me all along. She said once, 'I've been in this business for ten years and this snotty-nosed punk comes along and gets a show.' No matter what, to her I'm just the Antichrist."

Clearly, Will did not mince words—but as Will often does, after that first outburst, he calmed down and readdressed the situation more reflectively. The next time a reporter asked him about the "Aunt Viv" crisis, he gave a more balanced interview. In part, he said, "Janet Hubert-Whitten was an incredible actress. She brought so much spirit and fun and warmth to *Fresh Prince*. She made that set a home. She was really special. Of course, there was pain in her leaving, but she thought it was me, which kind of irritated me, but people make their own beds and have to sleep in them. I didn't have anything to do with it. She just never believed that."

Will may or may not have had a hand in Ms.

Hubert-Whitten's firing; he certainly had a major voice in the hiring of her replacement. Midway through the *Prince*'s reign, Will had earned his Executive Producer stripes and in that capacity, huddled with producer Winifred Hervey-Stallworth to find a new "Aunt Viv."

Their choice was Daphne Maxwell Reid, who had co-starred with her husband, Tim Reid, on the series *Frank's Place* and appeared in the series *Snoops*. The *Fresh Prince* cast was familiar with Daphne's work, and with her sunny-side-up reputation. They were psyched about her coming aboard.

For her part, Daphne had her own concerns. "I was afraid of being known as the 'replacement,'" she'd said. "I thought there would be strain, like my being a stepmother." Those worries were quickly dashed after just a few weeks of work, as Daphne glowed about her new comrades. "These people opened their arms and their hearts. It was like they wanted me there and treated me so well. I came in fresh and uninformed. Now, it feels like I've been a part of that family all along. We just have a ball."

On screen, and in typical *Fresh Prince* style, there were no uncomfortable pauses when a very different-looking actress arrived to start the season as Aunt Viv. Only Jazzy Jeff made an on-camera comment about her sudden appearance. "You sure have changed since you had that baby," Jeff quipped. That was all that was ever said—it was all that had to be said. The audience embraced the new Aunt Viv as lovingly as the cast had. They also embraced little Ross Bagley, who joined the cast soon after as little cousin Nicky, Aunt Viv and Uncle Phil's new addition.

Things were as close to perfect on *Fresh Prince* as could be. The characters Will and Carlton had graduated prep school and were now freshmen at the fictional University of Los Angeles, which opened up all sorts of new storylines and situations: an apartment for the boys, a new girlfriend for Will, and even new sets.

But the real-life Will still had an itch to be scratched—he was looking for his next film role. And he wasn't afraid to reach for the stars. When the cast was being selected for *Batman Forever,* Will wanted the role of Robin so much he could taste it. He told his agent, he told his friends, he even told reporters that he wanted the part. But in the end Chris O'Donnell was chosen to slip on the Boy Wonder suit. Though Will was disappointed in losing the role, he took it in stride. By that time in his career, he really did believe that when one door closed, another opened. He may have lost out on being a movie good guy, but that only opened the door for him to become a very, very Bad Boy!

Chapter 8

Bad Boys

The movie that Will did get was the one that would put him on the fast track to blockbuster big-screen success. It was, of course, *Bad Boys*. An action-comedy, *Bad Boys* was an over-the-top buddy movie, tailor-made for two hot stars with outrageous personalities. One of the reasons Will said "count me in" so quickly was that the other star had already been cast: an equally hot, equally outrageous comrade in TV comedy, Martin Lawrence, star of his own self-titled sitcom. Although the two had never met, Will himself was a fan and had often thought about working with Martin.

But there were other reasons on Will's checklist for becoming a *Bad Boy*. In a very real sense, it marked the next logical step up the movie ladder for him. *Six Degrees of Separation* had brought him respect, but it was still a small, quirky movie, seen by a limited few. Now was the time to go for the gold, and *Bad Boys* was big-budget all the way. Another reason was the chance to play against type once again. "My role in *Bad Boys* is completely different from anything I have ever done," Will said. "He is a playboy and I have never been a playboy. On screen and in real life, I've always been the guy who couldn't get the girl. I like the change and I like the stretch. I went from *Fresh Prince* to *Six Degrees* and back to *Fresh Prince* and now to *Bad Boys*. I enjoy doing different things and trying to keep the audience off balance. I really like that a lot."

And not least of all, Will read the script and loved the plot instantly!

Bad Boys was set in Miami, Florida, and filmed on location there. Martin took the role of Marcus Burnett while Will played Mike Lowrey. Partners, they were top cops in the sun-city's elite narcotics division. In the beginning of the film, the heroic pair are basking in the glory of pulling off a $100 million drug bust, the biggest in the police department's history. But a dark cloud quickly turns their sunny skies into a hurricane of murder, mayhem, and madness. The captain summons the partners to tell them that someone has stolen their confiscated booty right out of the station's evidence room. And *their* jobs are on the line unless they get it back!

Though Marcus and Mike are longtime partners and good friends, they are exact opposites. Marcus is a happily married, somewhat mild-mannered father of three children who drives a staid family Volvo station wagon. Mike, on the other hand, is a Porsche-driving, free-wheeling bachelor, who dresses with style and flash and lives in a fabulous high-rise apartment. He comes from a wealthy family and grooves on the lifestyle.

When a beautiful girlfriend of Mike's is enlisted to go undercover to help find out information on the crooks, disaster strikes. She is killed and her innocent bystander best friend, Julie (played by Tea Leoni), is a witness to the horror. Julie was just visiting from out of town, and knows no one in Miami. She does know, however, that the killers are after her, so she seeks out the one cop she's heard her late friend talk about, Mike Lowery. In desperation, Julie calls the police station, insisting she has information about a murder, but will *only* talk to Mike Lowery. Unfortunately, Mike isn't there at the moment, so Marcus gets on the phone and pretends *he* is his partner.

As the movie progresses the pals have to keep up the switcheroo—naturally, there are hilarious consequences as one tries to "be" the other. Along with Julie, they track down the high-tech criminals, dodge bullets, and nearly get whiplash from high-speed car chases. A final showdown with their uber-thief quarry is choreographed with huge explosions and a sports car race to the death—with Volvo-driving Marcus at the wheel! Of course, the good-guy "bad boys" end up victorious as they ride off into the sunset as all good heroes do. And naturally, "the end" doesn't really mean *Bad Boys* is over: The path to a sequel is well-marked in the original movie.

As he'd done for *Six Degrees of Separation,* Will threw himself into preparation for his new role. The lanky rapper worked out diligently with a personal trainer. He lifted weights, he changed his eating habits, he hit the gym for three months so he could add some definition and cuts to his chest and shoulders. Why all the hard-body concentration? "As much as it is a movie, it's real, too," Will explained about the strain on the body in making a movie. "There is a lot of physical work that goes into it."

But the buffest bod and the most intense preparation would have meant zilch if Will and Martin hadn't clicked on screen as partners. Though the matchup seemed like a natural on paper, no one knew for sure if it would work until the two actually met. Any fears of them not getting along were dispelled within the first two minutes of their introduction. Martin, who got top billing in the film, remembers, "When I met Will, there was an immediate chemistry between us, and I knew that if we could get that chemistry on camera, we'd be cool. We opened our hearts to each other and decided, yeah, we could be partners."

Will wholeheartedly agreed. He observed of the electricity between them, "I think the key to a good partnership is developing that mental link where you can just look at someone and know what's up. It's Will and Martin, but it's a real action movie with some really good action sequences. Working with Martin was great. He's a comedic genius; in fact, he's a comedic geyser. We'd never worked together before, but it never felt like we were strangers—we got to really know each other. The chemistry was really great."

It was the chemistry of the two TV stars that excited movie studio bigwigs. At first glance, the *Bad Boys* script may have been dismissed as "just another cop-buddy film." But with Will and Martin top-lining, the buzz was on. Even before it opened, the word around town was that *Bad Boys* could be as popular as the biggest buddy movies— like Mel Gibson and Danny Glover in *Lethal Weapon* or Nick Nolte and Eddie Murphy in *48 Hours;* in other words, a match made in celluloid heaven.

If the pairing of Will and Martin didn't ensure long lines of their fans at the box office, the genius promotion of *Bad Boys* did. For weeks before the film opened, TV commercials ran of Marcus and Mike arguing back and forth as they drove along a Miami highway, breaking into a very off-key rendition of the reggae theme song of the *Cops* TV series. "Bad Boys . . . Bad Boys . . . whatcha gonna do . . ." the two crooned. The strategy worked. Like the song of the mythical Sirens, they led a mesmerized audience to break all sorts of first-week box-office records. *Bad Boys* made a splash heard from Hollywood to New York. It was 1995's first out-of-the-park home run.

The reviewers agreed with the viewers. *Entertainment Weekly* assessed the teaming of the two as top-notch casting. "There's a spark of canniness in casting Lawrence and Smith against type. Smith, the clean-cut sitcom prince, plays the swinging bachelor, and Lawrence, notorious for the raunchiness of his stand-up routines, is the devoted family man. . . . Lawrence and Smith are winningly smooth comic actors. Smith especially holds the camera with his matinee-idol sexiness and his quicksilver delivery of lines such as 'You're driving almost slow enough to drive Miss Daisy!'" *People* magazine praised, "The unfailingly ingratiating Smith glides through the movie . . . Smith is an actor with a refined sense of comedy. He is also physically imposing enough to pull off a serious action film." Even *Rolling Stone* was impressed and, in describing the final scene, wrote, "The climatic shootout inside an airplane hangar, complete with a 727 blowing sky high, slides the film into overdrive. It's all special-effects noise and nonsense. We're not fooled. Lawrence and Smith are the real firecrackers."

When the cash register finally stopped *kerchinging, Bad Boys* ended up grossing $140 million domestically and another $75 million overseas—and that didn't count the tally from video sales and rentals, which is still adding up. And say what you will about reviews and respect, when it comes to Hollywood powers-that-be, box office is what impresses them. The "big boys and girls" with the Hollywood clout took notice of Bad Boy Will Smith in a way they never had before. The new Hollywood perception of Will was that his name on a movie marquee could ensure a hit. Which isn't a bad way to be perceived!

Once again, Will had made the right career

move, and once again, it had paid off in more than one way. Personally, he'd made a lifelong friend in Martin Lawrence, a bond he will always cherish. Professionally, well, it doesn't get any better: This new chapter in his career resume would lead to bigger and better movies to come, including the very strong possibility of a sequel. There was one other upshot to the titanic success of *Bad Boys*. It helped him make a tough decision, one he'd been mulling over for a long time.

Chapter 9

The Prince Abdicates

All good things must come to an end, and *The Fresh Prince of Bel Air* was no exception. As Will and the rest of the cast were heading into the 1995–96 season, the decision was made that it would be the last. That decision came right from the top, right from the Prince himself.

"I felt like it was time to end the show," Will told *Ebony* magazine. "We had a nice run. I had done movies like *Six Degrees of Separation* and *Bad Boys,* I was up for more—including *Independence Day*—and the TV show just felt confining. You're pretty much one character, and there are not many peaks and valleys, just pretty much the same old, same old. And I wanted to go out while we were still good. You get up to eight or nine seasons and then you're struggling. I wanted to go out solid, while we were still funny."

Clearly, from Will's point of view, the decision made ultimate sense. But that doesn't mean it was made lightly. Will understood that ending the show affected not only his own life, but the entire cast and crew's: Not all of them were in the middle of big-movie fame. But Will had hung in for as long as he could. Truthfully, he'd been dropping hints about wanting to end the show ever since he made *Six Degrees,* some two years earlier. In an interview back then, Will confessed, "Artistically, the show has made me feel somewhat crazed, but I'll stick with it through the end of my contract."

At the same time Will confided to another reporter, "When I got into this business, the most important thing for me was to always try to stay on the edge. It's really difficult with television to be anywhere near the edge, especially Monday night at 8 P.M." That, of course, was back when the early time slot was considered "family hour."

If anyone was listening, the hints were there. Finally, though, Will decided to stop dropping clues and speak out—loud and clear. But in typical, sensitive Will fashion, he didn't go in and drop a bomb on the producers, he took the classy road. Will officially gave a full year's notice of his plans to "abdicate," which coincided with the completion of his contract. That meant he'd fulfilled his contractual obligations *and* given everyone else time to make future plans.

When the word was out publicly, Will handled the queries with professionalism and honesty. "It became increasingly difficult to find that guy inside me," Will explained. "All the things *Fresh Prince* stood for, all the fun he had, still exist inside me, it's just that those aren't the dominant aspects of my personality anymore."

Though Will had said at the 100th episode party he wanted to do 100 more shows, the *Fresh Prince* run fell a bit short. By the end of their last season, they had completed 149 shows—but they were 149 *good* shows the entire cast was proud to have credited to their resumes.

In a testament to how much affection his co-stars really had for Will, all of them were understanding and even quite supportive of his decision. Alfonso Ribeiro was very philosophical about it and summed up Will's departure with the understanding that "life goes on" and "everything changes." Alfonso realized that Will's personal life changes had made it impossible for him to continue on with *Fresh Prince* and maintain its quality. "So much in Will's life had changed, and it changed him," explained Alfonso. "But his TV role stayed the same." On a personal note, Alfonso expressed his gratitude that fate had brought Will Smith into his own life and, with a tip of the hat, added, "It's been great to have him as a brother and a friend for all these years."

Tatyana agreed, adding that she had grown as an actress and as a person from her years on *Fresh Prince.* "After we finally got close, Will became like a big brother to me—advising, helping, encouraging, protecting me," she recalled. She had seen Will grow, too, and was one hundred percent behind him when he had insisted on having more realistic storylines. That decision was very effective, Tatyana observed as she looked back on the *Fresh Prince* run. "From the fan mail I've received, I know the show helped many teens get through difficult situations in their lives. We've touched on real problems kids have—drug use, sex, prejudices, inner-city problems. Even if we couldn't offer them solutions, our show has shown them that they are not alone."

In March of 1996 the cast of *Fresh Prince* completed taping the final episode. It aired May 20, 1996. A heartwarming farewell from the fictional Banks family to all their friends and supporters, it blurred the line between "real life" and "reel life." In doing so, that last episode combined the very best ingredients of a sitcom: moments that tickle the funnybone and others that touch the emotions. The premise was about ending, and new beginnings. After Hilary and Ashley made plans to move to New York, the rest of the Banks family, Aunt Viv, Uncle Phil, Carlton, and little Nicky, decided to sell the house and move to the East Coast. Even Geoffrey, the butler, was returning to his roots in England. Only Will planned on staying in Los Angeles to finish college. Just before the Bankses left for a family trip back to Philadelphia, Aunt Viv and Uncle Phil put the house up for sale. Potential buyers flocked to the house—and because it was a natural situation for nostalgic jokes, those potential buyers included the families from TV sitcoms past, *The Jeffersons* and *Diff'rent Strokes*.

The wink-wink laughter was accompanied by

emotional moments, such as when Uncle Phil, Will's demanding but grudgingly loving guardian, reminisced about the day his nephew first arrived in Bel Air. "I remember a kid loaded with all the potential in the world, and now I see a person on the verge of realizing that potential," he said with tears in his eyes.

Viewers could tell by the catch in James Avery's voice as he said those words, he really, really meant them—for the reel-life *and* the real-life Will. There wasn't a dry eye in the house, on the set, or in the audience!

So, after six great seasons, the *Fresh Prince* set went dark for the final time. Everything was over, except for the celebrations. The cast and crew had much to celebrate and remember—and they did, big time. "After we taped the last episode," Tatyana described, "we had a final wrap party and I think I spent ten or fifteen minutes crying my eyes out, like everybody else in the cast, because it was all over."

There were tears, happy memories, hugs and kisses, touching speeches, and a wild and crazy cake fight! No one was spared. Will, Tatyana, Karyn, Alfonso, James, Daphne, Joseph, Jeff, and even little Ross Bagley all were wiping icing and crumbs from their hair and off their faces most of the evening.

Everyone had something to say, and it didn't matter what part you'd played in the show's success. Crew members got the same speech time as the stars; in a touching tribute, a cameraman got up and stated that of all the shows he'd worked on behind the scenes, the *Fresh Prince* set was truly one of the happiest ones in Hollywood. "Will kept everyone laughing even when the cameras stopped rolling," he said.

As the host with the most for the evening, Will made sure he talked with everyone who had anything to do with the show. He wanted to thank them all for six seasons of fun, moral support, and a great learning experience. "Everyone on this show is the best," he raved to a reporter who cornered him for two minutes. "The writers, producers, directors—the greatest cast in television. I respect them all."

Before the last sounds of laughter and music faded at the wrap party, Will gave a memorable eulogy to the show that had launched his career. He was proud of *The Fresh Prince of Bel Air* and wanted to go on record with his pride. "The audience related the character to reality. When I said a line, the audience didn't feel I was acting. What that allowed me as an artist was to more effectively carry my audience wherever I wanted them to go."

Will had come a long way from the first day he stepped on the *Fresh Prince* set and mouthed everyone else's words! The star recalled some of his best memories from *Fresh Prince*. They included some of the show's famous guest stars: Bell, Biv, DeVoe; Boyz II Men; Oprah Winfrey; Al B. Sure; Bo Jackson; Tyra Banks, to name just a few.

But Will took a moment to tip his hat to the most special guest star of all, the famous stage actor Ben Vereen, who played a pivotal role in one of the last episodes, one that Will feels is "the most powerful *Fresh Prince* ever."

Mr. Vereen portrayed the father who had walked out on Will and his family some fifteen years earlier. It wasn't an easy show to do. But in snaring Ben Vereen to play Will's father, the young actor explains that they'd struck gold.

"I thought it was very important to see something in the character who plays Will's father—to be able to see where Will got his charisma from. But there had to be another element as well. The father, after all, had deserted Will—the old man had to have a special quality so the audience wouldn't hate him. I thought that he really needed to be a character who was someone you could listen to . . . before you passed judgment. Ben Vereen is one of the only actors in Hollywood who could've made that character believable."

As an extra bonus of his experience working with the legendary star, Will declares, "I discovered a new level of depth in my acting ability."

There were many other favorite episodes that stand out in Will's memory, and he took the opportunity at the wrap party to reminisce about them. There was the one about his high school graduation being in jeopardy because he was missing credits in music. To be able to wear a cap and gown with his class, Will was forced to take makeup music lessons with a class of little kids. Needless to say Will made the whole experience funny, sweet, and especially memorable.

Another favorite was an episode called "Mistaken Identity." Will recalled, "My cousin Carlton and I were taking the car to Palm Springs for the weekend and got pulled over by cops." That one could have been taken straight from Will's many speeding experiences—accent on the "ex," of course. Will also cited the episode where Hilary dropped out of school and they had to "blackmail" her to get her back in.

Perhaps, though, the show Will was proudest of was "Just Say Yo." It aired in February of 1993 and was the first time the *Fresh Prince* writers dealt with the subject of teens and drugs. Will had campaigned for it the previous year, but the network nixed it. Finally, as Will gained more influence over the show, it was allowed to air.

"Just Say Yo" was about Carlton and Will's prom night. By accident, Carlton takes a pill he found in Will's locker. It had disastrous effects. A tearful and fearful Will admitted the perilous mistake of even having drugs in his locker—his biggest concern was that it hurt an innocent Carlton. The message wasn't merely to say no to drugs, but that just having drugs around can hurt you and those you love. It was a message heard by millions of kids watching their favorite sitcom.

So *The Fresh Prince of Bel Air* was over—at least in first-run. Even before Will and the gang said their farewells, the early episodes of *Fresh Prince* had been sold into syndication and were running with great success all over the world. In Spain it was the number one American series; in Germany it was number one in its time slot; in Italy and the United Kingdom it was the favorite show among kids and teens. In America, of course, the reruns continue to snag new fans with every episode. At the end of the day Will and the rest of the *Fresh Prince* cast walked away knowing they had put together a body of work that lives on.

But careers have to go on, too. Sometimes that's easier said than done. Tatyana admitted that the hardest part of saying goodbye at the wrap party was thinking about the future. "What will be toughest will be facing the end of the summer, knowing that I won't be back on the set with all my friends," she told a reporter.

As it turned out, for Tatyana and the rest of the cast, the future looked pretty good. The girl who'd grown up on screen as Ashley Banks spent most of that post–*Fresh Prince* summer enjoying herself, spending time with her boyfriend, actor Jonathan Brandis, attending premieres, dropping by a theater production Karyn Parsons produced, and getting ready for her senior year in high school by taking the SATs for college. Then she signed on to make an NBC TV-movie, *Fall into Darkness,* based on a Christopher Pike book. It co-starred her boyfriend Jonathan Brandis, and aired with super ratings in November 1996.

Karyn managed to ditch her Valley-girl Hilary persona, not only by doing live theater, but by spending some of the summer in New York City going to NYU film school. She returned to L.A. just in time to start a TV sitcom called *Lush Life.* Not only was she starring in it with her best friend, Lori Petty, but they were both producers of the show. Unfortunately, *Lush Life* was one of the first series to be canceled that season, but that didn't daunt Karyn. She just reversed gears and went into overdrive on several other projects.

James Avery and Alfonso Ribeiro had no time to wonder what they were doing next. Both landed new shows on the fledgling UPN network. The man who played gruff but lovable Uncle Phil now stars on *Sparks.* Alfonso, who played conservative Carlton, joined the cast of LL Cool J's *In the House* when it moved from NBC.

Little Ross Bagley, who was Nicky for two seasons, had several projects lined up, including a home video series called *The Garage Kids.* As for Jazzy Jeff, he kept busy with his own production company, called Touch of Jazz.

And then there was Will. Just as he won his "freedom" from *Fresh Prince,* he declared his *Independence Day* with what just might end up being the all-time biggest blockbuster movie ever!

Chapter 10

"Welcome to Earth!"

Forty-eight percent of Americans believe in UFOs. Twenty-nine percent of the U.S. citizenry believes we've already made contact with aliens. In April 1996 the governor of Nevada officially changed the name of Route 375 to Extraterrestrial Highway because so many people have sworn they have sighted UFOs there.

No wonder filmmakers have had such a field day making movies about UFOs and life in outer space. The success of movies and TV shows like *Star Trek*, *Star Wars*, *The X-Files*, *Dark Skies*, and *Millennium* prove that the public is fascinated with the idea of contacting alien life; the appetite for projects dealing with such phenomena seems insatiable. So when director Roland Emmerich and producer Dean Devlin—the filmmaking team behind the very successful movie *Stargate*—brought up the idea of a disaster epic about aliens attacking Earth, deal-makers at Twentieth Century Fox listened. They kept listening as the duo explained why their film was different from all previous cinematic space treks.

Recalling those preliminary meetings, Dean Devlin says, "Clearly the script had an appeal. I think we created what would be a wonderful 'What if?' scenario on an enormous, international scale. Everyone who read it recognized that we hoped to attempt something special, in terms of size, scale, and adventure."

The filmmakers were also insistent that this ensemble epic had to have a sense of humor. "We were adamant about that," Roland Emmerich says. "I think it's the only way to do something like this because otherwise it would be too dark, too depressing. That's why we like to also call it a 'popcorn' movie. We wanted to give people an exciting and fun ride."

The execs at Twentieth Century Fox agreed with the entire concept and, as they say in the biz, "green-lighted" the pic. *Independence Day* was born.

Casting for *Independence Day*, nicknamed *ID4* (because its climactic scene takes place on July Fourth), began. The three pivotal characters were the President of the United States, the computer genius, and the Marine jet-fighter pilot. It was crucial to pick the right actors for these roles.

Though many thought the filmmakers would have gone after proven action heroes like Arnold Schwarzenegger, Harrison Ford, Sly Stallone, or even Linda Hamilton, the duo behind *ID4* had other ideas. "When you have a movie with such a well-known big-action star," Mr. Emmerich explained, "you know his or her character will triumph. In our movie, everybody's fate is up in the air."

Jeff Goldblum (*The Fly II, Jurassic Park*) was tapped for the role of David Levinson, the computer genius; Bill Pullman (*Casper, While You Were Sleeping*) won the part of President Whitmore. Will Smith, fresh off *Bad Boys,* was chosen to play Captain Steven Hiller.

Together they were the "Brains," "Soul," and "Heart" of *ID4*.

Will couldn't have been more psyched about this new opportunity. He had proved his versatility with *Fresh Prince, Six Degrees of Separation,* and *Bad Boys,* but knowing the vicissitudes of showbiz all too well by now, he hadn't really counted on the chance to be in a movie this big quite yet. He figured on a few more steps up the ladder before he got to this point.

But the filmmakers felt strongly that Will was just the spark to the comedic, heartwarming aspect they had envisioned for *ID4*. They told the young actor that they were fans from way back—from his music videos, in fact—and had wanted to work with him for a long, long time. In true mutual admiration, Hollywood style, Will said he had grown up watching disaster films, so being cast in *ID4* was a dream come true.

In describing the movie itself, Will waxed eloquently—even if he did sound like a newspaper advertisement: "Thrills, chills, spills. You'll laugh, you'll cry. You never know who's gonna die. This is a disaster film in the classic sense, in the tradition of *The Poseidon Adventure* and movies like that. There's a threat that the planet is going to be destroyed and the aliens actually begin destroying it. It's warm, it's funny, it's chilling, all at the same time."

In spite of the hyperbole Will was pretty much right on. What *ID4* had going for it was a unique, and uniquely staged, combination of edge-of-your-seat excitement, special effects, humor (both cerebral and physical), suspense, and a whole lot of heart. It all revolved around characters, including an innocent little girl (and if that wasn't huggy enough, a heroic puppy) the audience instantly cared about.

Put more succinctly and in today's vernacular: *Independence Day* was, simply, all that.

Independence Day begins with the citizens of Earth leading their normal, everyday lives. Yes, there were wars, famines, natural disasters here and there, but nothing out of the ordinary was happening. Americans were preparing to celebrate a most joyous holiday, the Fourth of July, the day in history when they declared their independence from England.

But, without warning, something extraordinary

happened. Strange, huge shadows fell across major cities and country towns. As all eyes turned skyward, Earth was swept by ominous and unexpected upheavals of nature—tornadoes, earthquakes, hurricanes, tidal waves. But these disasters paled in the realization that the shadows and the weird phenomena were caused by enormous spaceships hovering over strategic parts of the globe. If anyone ever asked, "Are we alone in the universe?" they got the answer: NO!

Soon heads of state all over the world realized that in spite of their political differences, they had to band together to battle this ultimate enemy. New York, Los Angeles, Washington, D.C.—cities and their populace were being destroyed with a flash of alien fire. President Whitmore had to come up with a way to communicate with and stop the aliens and their deadly mission. Fate brought Whitmore together with a host of experts who had suggestions, ideas, and even prophecies, all to no avail. No one really knew how these seriously ugly bad-dude aliens were getting in, or how to stop them. In the end it had to be the combination of the President himself, computer genius David Levinson, and fighter pilot Captain Hiller—the soul, the brains, and the heart—who saved the Earth.

Will was determined to make *ID4* his *tour de force,* and he knew that research and preparation were the key. Well before principal photography began, he got ready for his role. He had never played a military man, much less a fighter pilot, so Will familiarized himself with the training that

Steve Hiller had gone through. He researched his character by studying the basics of flying an F-16 with a Marine lieutenant. He even took a spin in the Marines' "simulator," a device that allows the "pilot" to experience a flight in an airborne fighter jet while never leaving the ground. So when Will, as cigar-chomping, hooting 'n' hollering Captain Hiller roars off "to kick ET's butt," the audience really believes he could do it.

This opportunity intrigued Will, but the basic character of Captain Hiller is what held the most appeal. "He's interesting because he's definitely serious, but he's also able to be funny," Will observed. "I've never experimented with that before. It's either been one or the other."

A more compelling appeal of the starring role for Will was the fact he was an African-American hero. "I was happy to be a black man saving the world in *Independence Day*," he said. "Black people have been saving the world for years, only nobody knew it."

Will was most enthusiastic about filming the action scenes. He could barely keep silent about the sensational special effects he witnessed while filming *ID4*. When, in the weeks before the premiere, Will was finally allowed to talk about the movie to the press, he could not contain his excitement—he sounded like a little kid, with the level of enthusiasm he hoped the audience would have. "There's a scene where you see the Statue of Liberty falling over in slow motion," he marveled during an interview. "So, it's like, 'Oh, my God!' The special effects are so realistic, you feel exactly the way you would if something of this magnitude was ever to really happen."

And just how did the forces behind *ID4* create such fabulously realistic special effects? They used everything—old and new—that was available to them in FX (special effects) technology. It was a massive amount of work. The film, which reportedly cost $70 million to make, had three and a half months of principal photography (where the actors are on set), *ten months* of second-unit shooting (where the filmmakers fill in the rest of the movie's scenes) and nearly 500 computer-generated shots.

But the producer and director didn't rely *only* on computers and digital technology. "That's a fantastic tool," Dean Devlin claims, "but it's not for everything. There's a tendency to latch on to whatever new toy has been invented, but sometimes you need a good old-fashioned model on a string."

He continued, "There were times when we'd look at an action sequence and say, 'Yeah, it's good, but wouldn't it be great if this whole thing blew up and then he flew underneath it?'" So some scenes were a combination of high- and low-tech effects, with computer-generated explosions over plastic airplanes hanging on "invisible" strings. A perfect example was the scene where a wall of flames literally explodes down a skyscraper to a New York City street. "Who would have known it was a ten-foot model turned on its end with a flame at the bottom and the camera on the top?" Mr. Devlin asked, as he expanded on the technique. "Flame goes up, and if you film it from above and twist the image, you've got a wall of flame coming toward you. I love that kind of thinking. If you're clever enough, you can pull it off with cardboard and papier-mâché." Talk about low-tech!

Sometimes any type of technology made it strange for the actors. Since the special effects were added after the principal photography was done, it required a lot of "blue screen" scenes, which means the actors performed their scenes in front of a light blue screen, so the background could be technically filled in later. It also required a method called "acting blind." It was Will's first experience in this technique, and he recalls, "In a scene with an alien, you're talking to AIR or a sign that says ALIEN. For the cockpit scenes during the dogfights between military jets and spacecraft, the director stood off camera saying, 'There's an explosion to your left! Now the plane dips to your right!' . . . I heard all this and I was thinking, wait, I never knew this is what Han Solo went through in *Star Wars!*" Clearly, the magic of this kind of movie making was a little bit odd and even disconcerting for Will and his co-stars.

Not so disconcerting, of course, that it ever dashed Will's natural bent for the absurd. As usual, he kept everyone laughing with his antics. Whether he was cracking wise, lifting his movie son-to-be, seven-year-old Ross Bagley (who also played his cousin Nicky on *Fresh Prince*), over his head as a human barbell, or staging mock Ninja fights behind the scenes, Will was a farcical leader on the set. When things could have gotten tense, Will injected a healthy dose of humor into the situation. That humor sometimes caused explosions of its own: no FX needed. "We got into this laughing jag that doubled us over," Will recalls when he and Jeff Goldblum were flying off in an alien spacecraft to take on the Mother Ship. "It just suddenly struck us as so completely hilarious that life as we know it depended on Jeff Goldblum and Will Smith! I turned to Jeff and said, 'Man, this planet is in trouble. Give up now! Surrender!' "

Surrender—that's exactly what the other "boffo" 1996 summer films did in the wake of *ID4*, which took no prisoners in its march across the movie screens of America. While *Twister, Mission: Impossible, The Rock*, and *Phenomenon* were all big money-makers for the studios that summer, *ID4* ruled and left them in the dust. *ID4* opened in 2,400 theaters across North America, and in its first five days it became the highest-grossing film for that time period in history. Over the July Fourth weekend, it pulled in $83.5 million and in just six days, *ID4*'s total came to $96 million. After a little less than two months *ID4* inched toward the $300 million mark, making it second only to *Jurassic Park* in reaching that benchmark so quickly.

The movie received glowing reviews, and so did Will Smith, whose performance was not overshadowed by the special effects. One weekly news magazine declared, "With *Independence Day*, Will Smith goes from big star to really, really big star. His effortless charm and comic timing may not be the reason people are lining up for this movie, but he is the reason people are cheering at the end." The (then) twenty-seven-year-old actor even graced the July 8, 1996, cover of *Newsweek* magazine, which explored America's obsession with aliens, psychics, and the paranormal.

ID4's success was hardly just an American phenomenon. The overseas box offices were bursting at the seams, too. France had a record opening day with $2.3 million in ticket sales. In the United Kingdom *ID4* set the all-time opening weekend record with $10.9 million. The same was true for Australia, which saw *ID4* pulling in $7.75 million its opening weekend. Record premiere weekends were also set in Germany with $15.2 million, Austria with $1.1 million, Norway with $1 million, even Lebanon with $91,763 (it played in only 5 theaters there).

The only "hiccup" in *ID4*'s off-shore openings occurred in Spain when it opened in September 1996. As in the United States, there was a massive radio and TV campaign promoting *ID4*. The TV commercials showed a newscaster giving a report describing alien spaceships hovering over New York. However, hundreds of people didn't realize it was a commercial for a movie, and panic set in. Radio and TV switchboards were flooded with calls from fearful citizens thinking that a real attack had begun! Once the Spaniards were calmed, they, like everyone else, rushed out to see the movie.

After a little less than three months in European theaters, *ID4* had earned its studio bosses the huge sum of $174.3 million. And by the middle of October 1996 non-American ticket sales added up to a whopping $318.6 million.

When all the receipts—including those anticipated for video sales and rentals (the video was released in November 1996)—are tallied, the movie is expected to fly by even *Jurassic Park,* to become the second most profitable in Hollywood history. Which was the first? It took a King to outpace the Prince: King Simba, that is. Only *The Lion King* has so far proved more profitable than *ID4.*

The *ID4* story doesn't stop there. Already there is talk of a possible sequel (*ID4-2? ID5? ID4 with a Vengeance?*) for the summer of 1998. And insiders say that if the go-ahead is given, Will Smith will be the first actor they sign up. They'd better hurry—Will's movie dance card is filling up fast.

All You Need Is Love

If Will's career has been a steady upward climb, he hasn't been quite that lucky in his private life. Of course, no amount of strategy, ambition, risk-taking, and determination can guarantee a successful love life. That, after all, is a matter of the heart. And there's nothing rational when it comes to emotions. Still, Will hasn't exactly been unlucky in love.

Unlike the freewheeling characters he often plays, Will himself is not a "player" and never has been. "I've always been a one-girl guy," he has revealed. "I don't know why, I just prefer to be with one person."

Even back in high school the "Clown Prince" got serious when it came to the ladies. "I've never been

out there trying to find a different girl every night,"
Will said of his teenage years. "I've almost always
had a girlfriend." His standards for a girlfriend
haven't changed much over the years. "I like an
intelligent woman. I like an independent woman
who has her own identity that I can respect."

In the years since high school Will has found
three women who measured up to that description
and who, at various times, have captured his heart.

The first real love of Will's life was Tanya Moore,
a college student who was nineteen when he met
her in 1988. That year was also Will's first brush
with superstardom. He'd won a Grammy and was
in the middle of sold-out appearances across the
country in support of *He's the DJ, I'm the Rapper*.
It was also Will's year of "behaving badly." Only,
when he met Tanya, the downside hadn't hit him
yet. He was on an absolute high. He had fame,
fortune, and was having plenty of fun.

When DJ Jazzy Jeff and the Fresh Prince arrived
on the campus of San Diego State University to
perform that year, Will had no idea his life was
about to take a love detour. But when he saw
beautiful student Tanya Moore in the audience, his
heart skipped a beat. After the show Will made
sure he got himself introduced to Tanya. During
their first conversation, he found out she was a
business major. Tanya had beauty and brains: She
fit Will's "dream girl" description and he didn't
hesitate to tell her. As Tanya has said of that first
encounter, "Will just came right up to me and said
I was the girl of his dreams."

Tanya was surprised, to say the least, at Will's

forthrightness, but agreed to a date. One date led to another, and their relationship slowly progressed. Tanya ended up being one of the many people who helped Will spend his mad money that whirlwind first year, but she was also one of the few who stuck by him when it was all gone.

She was there, too, for the beginning of the *Fresh Prince*'s TV reign. During that time, Will's burgeoning fame led a bevy of starlets to his door, but he ignored them all for Tanya. She became, in fact, "one of the guys." At least that's the way he described her to a *People* magazine reporter in one of his first interviews for the publication. Will said, "We just hang out. What's good about Tanya is that she thinks like a guy, so I don't miss my buddies. It's like, I can't relate to somebody crying because she broke a fingernail."

If Will sounded less than mature, remember, he was barely out of his teens at the time. For her part, Tanya was her own woman, with her own independent identity. Will never felt he had to be her whole life. Tanya enjoyed Will's success, but seemed to know and love the down-to-earth dude beneath the veneer of stardom. "Will is real cool about everything," she'd explained in that same magazine interview. "He's like none of this has hit him."

Their relationship lasted three years—a Hollywood eternity. But early in 1991 something went wrong. Much to the surprise of Will's friends, fans, and family, Will and Tanya broke up. The gossip was that Will's nonstop schedule had affected their relationship; it was also tattled that Tanya had started dating New Edition's Johnny Gill. Some insiders leaked that Will was so brokenhearted, he went into a tailspin, which led him directly into a rebound relationship with aspiring fashion designer Sheree Zampino.

Speculation is pretty much all anyone had to go on. For just as Will maintained a discreet silence about other breakups in his life, he did not reveal many details about this one, either. Of course, that didn't stop the press from asking what went wrong. While Will's reply didn't pinpoint Tanya, he did cite the "green monster" as a breakup cause. "When I got famous, women started looking at me differently. The girl I was with, no matter how much we were in love, just couldn't accept the fact that other women were looking at me and screaming at me onstage. And love just couldn't beat life, not in my situation."

Whether Tanya got jealous, or started dating someone else, the world will never know. But anyone with an eye on Will knows exactly what came next in *his* life—and really quickly—love, and marriage.

Will and Sheree Zampino's initial introduction was pure Hollywood. In 1991 a mutual friend was appearing on the TV sitcom *A Different World,* and both Will and Sheree were in the audience to see an episode being taped. Later they went backstage to congratulate the friend. That's when Will took a long, hard look at Sheree. He was instantly captivated by her exotic looks and her down-to-earth personality. By that time he was quite famous; she was not intimidated at all. Indeed, as they talked, it became clear that Sheree could match him wisecrack-for-wisecrack. She was witty, beautiful, and, as it turned out, not easily won over. Later, Will would claim it was love at first sight for him; Sheree never said that.

They did not start dating right away. It would take six long months for Will to win Sheree over. He did it via a series of phone calls that led to a friendship. It was a relationship that might have started out slowly, but as soon as that friendship morphed into romance, it seemed to veer right into the fast lane. For Will was thinking marriage, and before the year was up, he proposed.

"It was Christmas Eve," Will has told of his romantic proposal to Sheree. "She was in Los Angeles and she thought I was flying to Philadelphia to spend Christmas with my family. What I actually did was go to the airport to meet my brother. He had flown in specially just to bring me a diamond ring I'd bought from a friend back East. I got the ring and went home. Then I called Sheree, pretending I was still at the airport. I told her I'd forgotten some really important papers. Could she go to my L.A. home, grab them, and bring them to me at the airport? She agreed, but of course, when she got to my house, there I was with the ring. I got down on one knee and proposed."

Not many women could turn down a romantic surprise like that, and Sheree didn't. She and Will married on May 9, 1992. Their wedding, at an exclusive hotel in Santa Barbara, was lavish—it set them back some $50,000. But who can put a price on happiness? And up to that point in Will's life, that day was his happiest ever. The wedding reception featured fabulous food, tender toasts, and the company of 125 friends and family members. Will's ring-bearing brother Harry was his best man. There were famous faces as well, including those of Jazzy Jeff, Denzel Washington, and Magic Johnson. All bore witness not only to the ceremony, but to Will and Sheree's wedding cake–smearing antics, all done in loving fun. The newlyweds and their guests partied well into the night.

That happiness seemed to grow day by day. Will and Sheree seemed a perfect match. Sheree often visited Will on the *Fresh Prince* set where co-stars and crew remember being entertained by the couple's back-at-ya' repartee. Sheree sometimes sat in on Will's backstage interviews, and added her own pithy comments. Will would just beam with pride, and explain, "Sheree and I got this comedy battle going!"

Will beamed even more brightly the day he and Sheree announced to the world that they were going to be parents. "This is the most exciting thing," Will burbled, "our baby is going to be a real-life prince or princess of Bel Air!"

When Will and Sheree's bouncing baby boy, Willard C. Smith III, nicknamed Trey, was born in the late fall of that year, Will was flooded with all sorts of emotions and expressed them as best as he could to the waiting press. "When the doctor handed me my son, it was this Big Explosion," Will described. "Suddenly I felt this huge yoke of responsibility. Being a dad changes everything. I suddenly realized things had to be different now, starting on the car ride home from the hospital. I made a vow to stay healthy, eat right, because it's not just for me anymore."

Trey became the center of Will's universe. He was determined to give his son everything his parents had given him: unconditional love, upstanding morals, and good values. "As Trey grows up," Will once said, "I hope he'll be proud of my work ethic and how I treat people. I always try to be nice, try to be positive. Children learn by example and I'm trying to set a good example for my son. I want to be the world's greatest dad in the eyes of my son."

To help make that happen, Will spent as much time with the new baby as possible. Sheree visited the *Fresh Prince* set ever more frequently, and as the seasons went by, Trey's smiling face became almost a backstage fixture. As the little prince grew from infant to toddler, he learned proper on-set behavior. The little boy was always very respectful, and he never whined or demanded special attention, even though he had to realize that his daddy was the star. But if Trey wanted to play with something, he always asked politely for permission first. And when the red lights went on, indicating that taping was about to begin, Trey knew that meant "quiet on the set." "Ssshh!" he would whisper, putting his finger up to his mouth.

Will, Sheree, and Trey seemed every bit the picture-perfect family. But looks can be deceiving, especially in Hollywood, where little is what it seems. Which is why Will's fans, and several of his friends, too, were shocked when he and Sheree, citing irreconcilable differences, announced their split in 1995. They announced it publicly and definitively in the press hoping to scoop the rag-mag tabloids. In spite of whatever private hurts they were nursing, they opted for a dignified public display and put on a united front. There was no rancor. For the most part, Will took the rap for the split. He admitted that maybe he and Sheree had rushed things, but offered no specifics. "When you don't know enough about yourself, you can't know someone else," he said a bit cryptically.

Sheree did not contradict him. She only said, "We were young, but we have a beautiful baby. Everything is cool—it worked out."

The divorce lawyers got to work, and in this aspect of the split, Will and Sheree were powerless to stop the tabloids, who had a field day with stories about the settlement. According to reports, Will ended up paying Sheree a lump sum payment of close to a million dollars, plus $24,000 in monthly alimony and child support. It was a lot of money, but Will reportedly agreed to it quickly. He wanted to make sure that Trey and Sheree would not want for anything.

Although the tabs were all over the story, they did not get any quotes from the divorcing parties. Both Will and Sheree took the high road. Their marriage just did not work out, and that was that.

Later on, a more reflective Will did comment on the divorce, in the course of a lengthy profile in a national magazine. He neither finger-pointed nor got specific, but drew an analogy anyone could relate to. "You know how you're on the freeway and you see that one car on the side of the road?

Thousands of cars drive by it. Well, every once in a while, it's your turn to be broken down. And you wait for the tow truck to come. That's how I view that difficult time in my life."

Of course, his own divorce was not the only one that ever affected Will. He, too, was a child of divorce. But just as his parents had maintained civil ties with each other, and more important, just as each parent stayed very involved in the lives of their children, Will aimed for a similar amicable new lifestyle. He and Sheree did remain publicly respectful of each other. They share custody of Trey, and Will is a very active and loving dad. It's obvious that Trey, now five years old, has inherited a lot of his dad's traits. The boy is, according to published accounts, a nonstop talker and doesn't seem one bit uncomfortable in the spotlight. In fact, photographers had a field day at the *Bad Boys* premiere, when Will and Trey turned up in matching white suits, black turtlenecks, and requisite Hollywood sunglasses. Father and son were the hit of the evening.

With the demise of his marriage, Will was not looking to fall in love again, nor did he expect to. But life rarely takes you where you expect it will. Within a year of his divorce, Will was waxing eloquently once again about love: Her name is Jada Pinkett. Like Will, she is an actor; like Will, she is a survivor of more than one busted-up romance. To Will, and way before they hooked up, she was a friend. They have known each other for seven years.

Ironically, Jada had "tried out" for the position

of Will's girlfriend once before, only to be turned away. Her tryout, however, was on-screen. Way back in 1990 Jada was one of several actresses who auditioned for a role in *The Fresh Prince of Bel Air* as Will's TV girlfriend. Her diminutive stature kept her from the part. The producers just didn't think petite Jada, who stands an even five feet tall, would look good next to Will's six-foot-three frame. Will and Jada laugh about that now. In real life, they look up to each other.

Jada was born in Baltimore on September 18, 1971, to a hardworking family not unlike Will's. Her dad was an independent contractor; her mom the head nurse at an inner-city clinic. Like Will, too, Jada was a natural performer. She studied her art through dance and choreography lessons at the Baltimore School of the Arts, and majored in theater at The North Carolina School of the Arts. A move to Hollywood to pursue her career landed her in the sitcom *A Different World* (no, she wasn't the mutual friend Will and Sheree had come to see that day).

Jada was proud of her work on the sitcom. Like Will, she took the responsibility seriously and looked to infuse the show with morals and messages in addition to the jokes and pratfalls. "We all worked very hard to give the show substance," she described. "Too many kids spend more time watching TV instead of reading books. *A Different World* was a program that not only took place in an educational environment, but where the characters were young people who cared about their futures. Hopefully, we served as good role models."

As Will had done, Jada moved from TV to movies. She has been in *Menace II Society, The Inkwell, A Low Down Dirty Shame, Jason's Lyric, Demon Knight,* and most recently, *The Nutty Professor* (with Eddie Murphy) and *Set It Off* (with Queen Latifah). A talented director as well, Jada took the helm of R&B singer Gerald Levert's video "How Many Times."

By 1995, when Will's marital world came apart, he turned to Jada—in her capacity as a friend only. It just so happened that she, too, was reeling from a romantic wreck, and they helped each other through the pain. "I helped him understand what had happened in his marriage," Jada told a reporter, "and he helped me see what happened in my relationships." With that, their own relationship suddenly took a more serious turn. "He's become my best friend," Jada has said. "There's nothing I can't say to him, nothing I can't share. He's smart, spiritual, sensitive."

When Will talks about Jada, it sounds as if he's found a soul mate. "She's intelligent, she's very in touch with her emotions, which allows me to be in touch with mine. She helps me deal with everything. No matter how difficult it gets, she always has something kind to say or a warm hug, or she'll cry with you if you feel like crying. She's someone I can talk to about anything. I've never been able to step outside my maleness to share myself with someone. She's the first person with whom I've been able to break that down. It's the first time I've truly known that a person outside my family loved me. She's the first person I've been with who's willing to accept that it's not always going to be great. But that's okay."

Jada also represents the first serious relationship Will has had with someone who truly understands the demands and the ups and downs of his career. They not only work in the same industry, but also share similar dreams and goals. Both are looking to long-term film careers—in fact, both are on the way to big-screen superstardom. Jada is already working on her new movie, about "a blind date from hell," titled *Woo*. Will, of course, is in for the long haul with sequels to his blockbuster films, and new roles to tackle as well.

Whether this relationship ends up long- or short-term is anyone's guess. But Will's fans wish him the best in his personal life, and right now, Jada Pinkett seems to be the best thing that has happened to him.

Chapter 12

Up Close and Personal

Where does Will go when the director yells, "It's a wrap!"? At the end of the day, like most working folks, he heads home. Admittedly, Will's home is not exactly on the same scale as that of most working folks. In the course of Will's superstar ascent, his bank account naturally swelled. And this time he was careful with his money, set aside plenty for taxes, and invested well. One of those investments was the home of his dreams.

Will settled on an 8,000-square-foot south-western-style abode an hour's drive northwest of Hollywood. Getting home from work at the studio is a long haul, but Will feels it's worth it. "Every-one complains about the distance," he acknowl-

129

edged, "but you feel like you're away from L.A., and that's important."

Will's home is his personal retreat—and his castle. The Prince has filled it with accoutrements designed for his pleasure. If Will wants to relax poolside, he can stretch out on one of the chaise lounges strategically placed around a sparkling, kidney-shaped pool. Breakfast is often taken beneath the wide umbrella at a picnic table by the pool. Will's backyard vista includes acres of landscaped gardens with beautiful fountains and his own private eighteen-hole golf course. Will likes to take a few swings out there every day.

The inside of his palatial home is just as luxurious. Huge glass French doors lead directly from the pool to the den, a warm, woodsy room furnished with dark, overstuffed leather couches and armchairs, and decorated with African artifacts. The centerpiece of the den is an inviting, wood-burning fireplace, which Will loves to turn up on cool California nights.

Comfy couches notwithstanding, when Will has time just to chill, he is anything but a couch potato. He loves to shoot pool, play racquetball and basketball, bowl, play a round or two of golf. He also works out to stay in shape. To engage in any of these activities, Will never has to leave the house: All the equipment he needs can be found on the grounds.

Will doesn't live with Jada, nor anyone else, but he's not alone in his palace. His two brown and black Rottweilers, Indo and Zahki, are on hand to greet him when he gets home. Naturally, there are plenty of visitors to the Prince's lair. His sister Ellen and his brother Harry both moved to L.A. to be close to Will. Harry, in fact, went to college to study finance and now handles Will's accounts. Parents Caroline and Will Senior stop by often as well. Will's dad has remained a strong presence in his life. He often accompanies his son on promotional tours around the country. "It's all been a dream come true," says Willard Smith, Sr.

Clearly, Will's loyalty to family and good friends has remained steadfast. The superstar hasn't ditched those who stood by him in the hard times. Benny Medina remains a close associate, as does Quincy Jones. These days, the list of Will's loyal friends has grown to include his fans, many of whom have been supporters for close to a decade. And when he gets the opportunity to do facetime with fans, Will makes it a point to be gracious and accommodating. Unless he's unusually hurried or hassled, he always makes time for an autograph and photo op, and usually a conversation as well. The interface not only makes the fans happy, it touches Will's heart as well.

Another important part of Will's life is the time he spends giving something back. Will is especially sensitive to those who haven't had the same breaks in life as he has. And he has an extra-special place in his heart for children. That's why, when it came time to decide on what charitable causes to support, Will chose two that benefit kids. He works tirelessly for both.

In 1991, when Will was still a relative newcomer to Hollywood, he was asked to be part of a celebrity day at the MacLaren Children's Center's annual picnic. MacLaren is a haven for abused and neglected children who have nowhere else to go. The annual picnic not only raises the spirits of these kids, makes them feel special, and gives them hope, it also raises money for the facility itself. Being there made Will feel pretty special, too.

"It feels good to be here with these kids," Will said on his first visit to MacLaren. "There are a lot of smiles here today. It's real easy to make their day. As a celebrity, it's easy to forget how important it is to help out. I want to encourage others to do it."

So encouraged, Will took on another kid-centered cause. For two years running, he has been the master of ceremonies for the NBA Stay in School Jam. The benefit is a hands-on way to address and reverse the ongoing crisis of school dropouts. All during the year various National Basketball Association stars visit schools and community centers to rap with kids and encourage them to get a good education. The visits culminate in one huge charity event—the NBA Stay in School Jam—that brings in thousands of dollars to support stay-in-school programs all over the country. On that night Will puts on his MC duds and hosts live entertainment, celebrity hoop-shoot contests, and does lots of donation-collecting.

Will's sincerity and big-heartedness is what sets him apart from many of his celebrity peers. Will Smith recognizes that life is a circle, and we all touch each other. "I'm comfortable with my life," Will has said sincerely. "I just try to put out good energy and it comes back tenfold. If there's one thing I've learned, it's that good begets good."

Will appreciates every good thing that has happened to him along the way. He knows how hard he worked for it, but also attributes at least some of his good fortune to plain old luck, being in the right place at the right time. "When I look back, I see what it could have been like, the things that might have gone wrong. It's like if I slept late one day, or had taken an extra five minutes to tie my shoe, I wouldn't have been in the right place."

Will's humility extends to his assessment of his own appeal. The star who describes himself as "silly, fun-loving, sensitive, and strong," quips that the main reason people from eight to eighty call themselves fans has to do not with what's in his heart, but what's on either side of his head. "It's the ears," Will quips. "Americans have an ear fetish. Americans love people with big ears—Mickey Mouse, Goofy, and me."

Chapter 13

Men in Black—and Beyond

Back in 1993, when Will decided to take the biggest risk of his career and go for *Six Degrees of Separation,* he'd said that his main goal was to be accepted as a serious actor "so that Spike Lee and Steven Spielberg and 'the big boys' will want to work with me." Three years later, in 1996, he got the call he'd been waiting for. It was from Steven Spielberg, by many accounts Hollywood's most revered director (the creative force behind such legendary films as *Jaws, Jurassic Park,* and *Schindler's List*). Mr. Spielberg's company was producing a new science fiction flick titled *Men in Black.* According to Will, their phone conversation was short and to the point. "Steven just said, 'You have to do this movie. We don't even want to talk about it.'"

Will didn't. Those were words he'd been waiting years to hear. But to the minds of other Hollywood-ites, perhaps Will should have talked about it—or at least thought first before jumping in head first.

Why? For one thing, *Men in Black,* a sci-fi adventure with comedy, sounds . . . not very different from Will's last blockbuster, *ID4.* For another thing, the role Will plays, of a hypercompetent, good-guy cop recruited to deal with aliens, sounds . . . not very different from the role of hypercompetent good-guy fighter pilot recruited to deal with aliens. For, uh, yet another thing, Will's *Men in Black* character, Jay, is a flippant, cocky, smart-mouthed, but deeply good-hearted action hero, which sounds . . . you get the picture. But that's not all. In the end of this movie he saves the world, again!

Why would any actor agree to play such a can't-help-the-obvious-comparisons role? Why would Will, of all actors, who prides himself on taking different kinds of roles, thumbs-up this one? When that exact question was posed, Will's answer, "You can't say no to Steven Spielberg," was simple, perhaps deceptively so. Chances are, it was more than that.

Though Will didn't say it, there's a good chance that financial rewards played a part. Of *Men in Black*'s $80 million budget, Will's cut was reportedly $5 million. While it didn't put him in Bruce

Willis's or Denzel Washington's category, it did represent his hugest paycheck so far.

If *Men in Black* becomes as successful as Will believes, it will solidify his status as a big-time movie action hero, one of the first African-American men to be in that rarefied league. For Will, there's always been a certain pride in being first— and best—at what he does. That is nothing new. There was, too, the element of challenge, another concept that has always attracted Will. This time, it's more of a "can he top himself" kind of thing, as Will knows all too well that the *ID4* comparisons are bound to dog him. Will *Men in Black* outpace *ID4* at the box office? No one knows, but for Will, it sure will be fun to try.

But there's another possible reason Will jumped so willingly into *Men in Black*. Call it the Chris O'Donnell connection. Chris, of course, is the actor who got a role Will wanted: Robin in *Batman Forever*. Word was, when *Men in Black* was being written, the part of Jay was, in fact, "earmarked" for Chris. For one reason or another, Chris did not end up with the role—Will did. Sweet revenge? Or just the "everything that goes around, comes around" concept? Whatever, the irony wasn't lost on Will.

In the end, the most compelling reason of all that Will took *Men in Black* was that he just simply liked the script. And despite the surface similarities, within that script there were, of course, major differences between his two movies. While *ID4* was a sci-fi alien adventure with comic elements, *Men in Black* is, at heart, a comedy—an over-the-top comedy, in fact, not dissimilar in certain ways to TV's *3rd Rock from the Sun.* The script is actually based on a comic-book series.

In this movie aliens are not hovering over Earth, poised to annihilate it. They're already here, and have been for decades. Cleverly disguised as humans, they've left their home planets to live "normal, decent" lives and are, in fact, productive in all sorts of professions ("though not as many taxi drivers as you'd think," explains one character to Will early on in the film) on Earth. Moreover, these aliens are far above humans intellectually. They're credited with such inventions as Velcro, microwaves, even liposuction. To them, humans are considered pretty low on the galactic food chain. And, as opposed to *ID4,* where Will was out to "kick some alien butt," in *Men in Black* he, in fact, delivers some alien baby! "Congratulations, it's a lizard," he says in one hilarious scene.

Will plays James D. Edwards III, a New York City policeman, who is dedicated to his job and does it well. A fairly average guy, he certainly doesn't go for that "aliens are out there," mumbo-jumbo. During a routine bad-guy chase, however, he encounters a "perp" who nearly escapes his clutches by suddenly "growing" four-inch talons that protrude from the ends of his fingers. Though he uses them to dig deep gashes into Officer Edwards, in the battle, it is the cop who emerges victorious.

Unbeknownst to Officer Edwards, his "performance" has been recorded by an elite corps of government agents, the men of INS-Section 6, better known as the "Men in Black." Their mission is to "police and monitor alien activity on Earth," and now that James has had an actual encounter with one, they'd like him to join their forces. At first, James is cynical, until he visits the MiB (Men in Black, of course) headquarters, one of the places many aliens actually work. When James gets an eyeful, he can't help but be impressed: These aliens are really cool. Talons aren't the only things they can grow—they do all sorts of body parts, including hearts and heads.

James is eventually persuaded to join the elite corps of special agents. When he does, his "identity" must be forever altered, as is the case with all the other agents. All identifying marks, including fingerprints, are changed, even his name is truncated. From induction day on, he is simply "Jay" and no longer has a private life, not that he had much of one before.

As "Jay," he is teamed with a partner, the world-weary "Kay," played by Tommy Lee Jones. Together, the Men in Black find themselves in the middle of a deadly plot devised by intergalactic terrorists. Two warring alien factions are poised to annihilate each other. Earthlings aren't the target, only the caught-in-the-middle innocent bystanders. It's up to Jay and Kay to save the planet.

Also starring in *Men in Black* is Linda Fiorentino, as a brilliant young coroner who wins Will's affections—and just possibly a place on the team. Should there be a sequel, she could very well become the first Woman in Black.

Linda, Tommy Lee Jones, and the other cast

members of *MiB* got treated to a dose of Will-behind-the-scenes. He was in top form. To relieve the tension of the long shoot, and just because he's irrepressible Will, he'd often swipe several huge, hairy fake insects from the prop truck, sneak up behind an unsuspecting cast member, and stick them down the victim's shirt. Noncast member, but real-life brother Harry Smith, was a frequent visitor to the set, and he did not escape his brother's antics.

There are amazing special effects in *Men in Black,* though, as the director is at pains to point out (apparently, the *ID4* comparison is on his brain, too), "nothing blows up" in this movie. Still, there are major car stunts, including one where a car jumps up above the traffic in a tunnel, attaches itself to the sides and roof of the tunnel, and roars, upside down, outta there!

The aliens themselves, of course, represent the most inventive computer-generated and anima-tronic special effects. There's little question they will be seen on the Toys "Я" Us shelves this holiday season, as several companies are lined up to produce replicas. Actually, marketing for *Men in Black* was in full swing way before the filming completed. *Men in Black* fans will be able to relive the excitement via a CD-ROM 3-D game that features worldwide, online network play. Posters will proliferate, and a line of *MiB* inspired cloth-ing, including sweatshirts and tank tops, will be on the retail racks. There will be lunch boxes, sleeping bags, trading cards, even shoes.

It doesn't end there. Columbia Television has

committed to develop an animated TV series based
on the film, set to debut in the fall of 1997. All that,
coupled with a possible (okay, probable) sequel,
make *Men in Black,* released in the summer of
1997, more than a movie, or more than a career
move for Will. It's more like a franchise, one that
he most probably has a piece of.

But before Will can even think about a *Men in
Black* sequel, he has to attend to projects he's
already committed to. That includes *Bad Boys II,*
which reteams Will and Martin Lawrence. Filmed
recently in Miami, it promises more action, adventure, and broad-based comedy. It's due to come out
later in the year.

Beyond that, the world of entertainment is wide
open for Will Smith, and welcoming him with open
arms. His choices seem limitless, and right now he
seems to be focusing exclusively on a film career. "I
enjoy making movies. It allows you to be someone
different every time you step up to the camera,"
Will says. Will would like to step up to the camera
next alongside his lady love, Jada Pinkett, but so
far the pair have not found a project they like.

It's been speculated that Will may take the lead
in a live-action feature based on Bill Cosby's animated *Fat Albert & the Cosby Kids* TV series. Part
of the appeal of that one involves paying homage to
one of his mentors. Another, no doubt, is the fun of
putting on a fat suit, just like another idol, Eddie
Murphy, did in *The Nutty Professor.*

Of course, there's always the possibility that Will
may take a hiatus from the big screen and do
something else altogether. Much as he loves movie

acting, he has changed course before, more than once. He's been nothing if not "the prince" of reinventing himself, after all.

One area of showbiz that can be pretty well counted *out* is rap. Although Will once declared, "I'll always be a rapper," Will and Jeff's fifth and last album, *Code Red,* was released in 1993, and he hasn't performed a rap song since. Nor does he have any plans to return to that genre. The rap world he left isn't the same anymore. The music has changed and, in Will's opinion, not for the better.

"These days, the negativity and hopelessness of gangsta rap pulls my creativity down. Listen to the lyrics, with all this hateful stuff they say about black people and women. It glorifies ignorance, violence, and misogyny. I'm embarrassed to listen to that stuff with my girlfriend. It's all about hate, and that's one thing I don't understand. I like the fun raps we did a few years ago, where you listen to the words and feel like there is some hope out there. Because I don't think things are hopeless. I think it's a beautiful world and a fun world. Why can't our music reflect that feeling?"

Does that mean Will won't ever record again? Will doesn't rule it out entirely, but it sounds doubtful. "I might cut a song for a movie sound-track here and there," he's said, "but music is my past. Acting is my future."

That does not include acting in another TV show, however. In spite of all the good times he had on *Fresh Prince,* and all the good that show did, Will still feels TV is too limiting. "You know," he said recently, "TV is a medium designed for mediocrity, whereas when you're making a film, you have more of an opportunity to achieve aesthetic perfection, or as close to that as you can get. You just have time to work on it."

Although Will is still relatively young, he's already been around the biz long enough to know that no one is on top all the time. He's seen the career of his idol Eddie Murphy take a tumble from the top, and only recently return to movie glory. "It ain't always gonna be great," Will acknowledges. "You gotta be prepared to take the bad times with the good times. If it all ends tomorrow, it'll be okay, because all my experiences have led me to who I am. And being sure of who you are helps you get through."

Will Smith has never truly needed the accolades of the outside world to feel good about himself. That feeling comes from inside, from being sure of who he is, and being true to that person. That is something Will Smith has always been, and will always be.

Chapter **14**

The Fabulous Will Smith Fact File

Real Full Name: Willard Smith, Jr.
Birth date: September 25, 1968
Birthplace: Philadelphia, PA
Hair & Eye Color: Brown, brown
Height, Weight: 6'3" tall, 200 lbs.
Parents: Caroline and Willard Smith, Sr.
Sisters: Pam and Ellen
Brother: Harry
Lives: Los Angeles, CA

Favorites

Music: Mariah Carey, Bobby Brown
Movies: *The Nutty Professor*, action movies, anything by (directors) Spike Lee and John Singleton

WILL SMITH

TV Shows: He doesn't watch much
Book: *Before the Mayflower: A History of Black America*, by Lerone Bennett
Sport: Golf
Game: Chess and video games
Food: Burgers and fries; fried chicken
Snack: Frozen yogurt
Style: Will favors shorts, tank tops, and high tops

Roll the Credits

TV: *The Fresh Prince of Bel Air*, 1990–1996
Movies:
Where the Day Takes You, 1992
Made in America, 1992
Six Degrees of Separation, 1993
Bad Boys, 1995
Independence Day, 1996
Men in Black, 1997
Bad Boys II, 1997

Discography (Albums)

Rock the House, 1987
He's the DJ, I'm the Rapper, 1988 (triple platinum)
And in This Corner, 1989
Homebase, 1991
Code Red, 1993

Awards

Grammy: "Parents Just Don't Understand," 1989; "Summertime," 1991

American Music Awards: Best Artist and Best Album, rap category, 1989

NAACP Image Award: "Outstanding Rap Artist," 1992

Nickelodeon Kids' Choice Award: "Favorite TV Actor," 1991

NATO/ShoWest Award: for *Bad Boys,* 1995

And Now for Something Completely Different: Will recently became an investor, putting up his own money to back Spike Lee's independent movie, *Get on the Bus.*

If He Could Be a Superhero: "I'd be Superman, because he could fly and everyone likes him."

"And You Can Quote Me . . ."

Will on Will:

"Confidence is what makes me different from guys at home. I'm the one who always takes the risks."

On Being a Role Model:

"A camera or a microphone in your face is power, and you have to make sure that the things you say and the things you do aren't misconstrued. But I've never really had to change anything I do. I would never do anything to embarrass myself or my family. And morally, the way that I've grown up, the things I do tend to be acceptable to people."

Will's Advice to Fans:

"Always remember that the harder you work, the harder you'll be able to play later. Balance is what it's about. Me, I play very hard, but when it's crunch time, I shoot the ball."

About the Author

Jan Berenson is a freelance writer working in New York City who has written several other young-adult and adult titles.